Can Cindy get Champion to behave?

Champion hated to be behind other horses. When Cindy rode him in the mornings, she tried to avoid certain other colts entirely. Champion had very distinct likes and dislikes about people and horses. He wasn't above showing it sometimes with a good nip.

"Champion's rearing in the starting gate!" Samantha cried.

"Hold him steady, Ashleigh," Mike said.

"She's trying!" Cindy could hardly stand to watch. The starting gate was a dangerous place. If Champion reared and lost his balance in the narrow space of the stall, Ashleigh could be crushed against the side. If she fell, she could be trampled under the colt's hooves.

To Cindy's immense relief, Champion's head bobbed down in the gate. The next second the doors flipped open.

Don't miss these exciting books from HarperPaperbacks!

Collect all the books in the THOROUGHBRED series:

#1 *A Horse Called Wonder*

#2 *Wonder's Promise*

#3 *Wonder's First Race*

#4 *Wonder's Victory*

#5 *Ashleigh's Dream*

#6 *Wonder's Yearling*

#7 *Samantha's Pride*

#8 *Sierra's Steeplechase*

#9 *Pride's Challenge*

#10 *Pride's Last Race*

#11 *Wonder's Sister*

#12 *Shining's Orphan*

#13 *Cindy's Runaway Colt*

#14 *Cindy's Glory*

#15 *Glory's Triumph*

#16 *Glory in Danger*

#17 *Ashleigh's Farewell*

#18 *Glory's Rival*

#19 *Cindy's Heartbreak*

#20 *Champion's Spirit*

#21 *Wonder's Champion**

#22 *Arabian Challenge**

THOROUGHBRED Super Editions:

Ashleigh's Christmas Miracle

Ashleigh's Diary

Ashleigh's Hope

Also by Joanna Campbell:

Battlecry Forever!

Star of Shadowbrook Farm

* coming soon

THOROUGHBRED

CHAMPION'S SPIRIT

CREATED BY
JOANNA CAMPBELL

WRITTEN BY
KAREN BENTLEY

HarperPaperbacks
A Division of HarperCollins*Publishers*

📕 HarperPaperbacks
A Division of HarperCollinsPublishers
10 East 53rd Street, New York, N.Y. 10022-5299

This is a work of fiction. The characters, incidents, and dialogues are products of the author's imagination and are not to be construed as real. Any resemblance to actual events or persons, living or dead, is entirely coincidental.

ISBN 0-06-106490-4

HarperCollins®, 📕®, and HarperPaperbacks™ are trademarks of HarperCollins*Publishers* Inc.

Cover art: © 1997 Daniel Weiss Associates, Inc.

First printing: May 1997

Printed in the United States of America

Visit HarperPaperbacks on the World Wide Web at
http://www.harpercollins.com/paperbacks

❖ 10 9 8 7 6 5 4 3 2 1

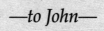

—to John—

CHAMPION'S SPIRIT

1

"CHAMPION, DON'T DO THAT!" FOURTEEN-YEAR-OLD CINDY McLean called in frustration. Her dad, Ian McLean, had just pulled the rearing, headstrong colt, Wonder's Champion, back down to the ground. It was almost post time for the Bashford Manor, a six-furlong race for two-year-olds at Churchill Downs. Ian, the head trainer at Whitebrook, one of Kentucky's premier Thoroughbred breeding and training farms, was trying to lead the colt around the walking ring before the race. So far Champion had fought him almost every step of the way.

Cindy shook her head. The track at Churchill Downs, home to the Kentucky Derby and famous for its white spires and classic elegance, was her favorite track in the country. Thousands of people had chosen to come to the races on this warm, summery day at the end of June. But Cindy's gaze was riveted to the showy Whitebrook colt, his supple muscles bunching under his sleek dark brown coat. His four white stockings flashed as he half dragged Ian around the ring.

"I hope we can get Champion to the track!" said Samantha McLean, Cindy's twenty-year-old sister. Her green eyes were full of worry.

"Maybe he'll settle down in a minute. Sometimes he just needs to work off his high jinks." Cindy wiped sweat off her forehead. She watched closely from the grass next to the walking ring as her dad tried to restrain Champion.

The magnificent dark brown colt bounced lightly on his front hooves. Shaking his almost black mane, he lunged toward the huge crowd surrounding the walking ring.

"Watch out!" cried a young man close to the horses.

Ian quickly stepped closer to Champion and pulled his head around. The colt huffed out a breath and jumped after his trainer.

"Champion, you just *have* to behave," Cindy said under her breath as he crossed in front of her.

The unruly colt seemed to hear. With a toss of his head he settled into a quick, spirited walk, his strides long and graceful.

Cindy relaxed just a little. Still, she itched to get

out there in the ring and try to control the colt herself. She knew that Champion went best for her. Unfortunately she wasn't old enough to lead him in the walking ring.

This wasn't the first time Champion had caused trouble at the track. In his maiden race three weeks ago the colt had acted up in the saddling paddock, the walking ring, and the gate. He'd won his first race by a nose, but after a difficult trip. Cindy was sure that Champion had won that race only because Ashleigh Griffen, Champion's jockey and co-owner of Whitebrook with her husband, Mike Reese, had expertly ridden the colt, maneuvering him out of trouble.

"Nothing's easy with Champion, is it?" Samantha asked.

"No." Cindy sighed. Champion's training had certainly had its ups and downs. Cindy had worked with Champion his entire life. He was the beautiful son of Ashleigh's Wonder, Ashleigh's champion race mare. Cindy had helped wean Champion and had been the first person ever on his back. Since last fall she had ridden him on Whitebrook's mile track, preparing him to race.

Champion had more talent on the track than any Thoroughbred Cindy had ever ridden, and she had ridden some of the best Thoroughbreds in the world at Whitebrook. The problem, she knew, was getting

3

Champion to use that talent. For a while she thought she had gotten the colt over his problems, but that hadn't been true for the past couple of months. The colt seemed to enjoy acting up just as much as running.

The five other horses in the six-horse field for the Bashford race were walking gracefully around the ring. Champion was high-stepping, vigorously yanking on his lead line, and snorting.

"None of these horses have raced much, have they?" Cindy asked Samantha.

"No, they're all two-year-olds—they're just getting started," Samantha replied. "But Duke's Devil, the black colt just ahead of Champion in the ring, won his first race convincingly in California last month."

Those colts don't have any more experience on the track than Champion, but they're all behaving a lot better than he is, Cindy thought. *He'd better cut it out!*

With a sudden squeal Champion rushed at Duke's Devil. The black colt's handler barely managed to pull him away in time.

"Clear the walking ring," the announcer blared.

Cindy cringed with embarrassment as everyone else led their horses out of the ring, leaving Champion by himself. The colt looked a bit bewildered, she thought. He didn't seem to understand what he had done.

"Bring him over here," Ashleigh called as she

4

walked into the ring. She wore the blue-and-white racing silks of Whitebrook.

"Mind Ashleigh," Cindy warned Champion as she and Samantha joined the colt at the far side of the ring. Champion's eyes glittered with excitement. He urgently bumped Cindy with his nose.

"You terror," Ashleigh said affectionately. "You know what's coming, and you want to get out on the track." Mike gave Ashleigh a boost into the small, light racing saddle.

Cindy was glad that Champion's antics didn't seem to be bothering his jockey. Now twenty-six, Ashleigh had ridden Ashleigh's Wonder, Champion's dam, to victories in the Kentucky Derby and Breeders' Cup Classic when she was just sixteen. Ashleigh was considered one of the best jockeys in the country.

"I can't wait till I'm old enough to ride at the track," Cindy said, looking up at Ashleigh. "Maybe I can ride Champion in a race!"

Champion danced sideways and ducked his head, trying to pull the reins through Ashleigh's hands. Ashleigh smiled wryly as she struggled to control the colt. "Be careful what you wish for, Cindy," she said. "You might get your wish."

"You'd better take Champion out to the track before the rest of the field gets here," Mike warned.

"Will do." Ashleigh pointed Champion at the tunnel to the track.

"Good luck!" Cindy said.

Champion twisted his head around to see her. Ashleigh straightened him out again, but suddenly he was fighting her every step of the way.

"I think he'd rather stay with you, Cindy," Samantha said with a smile.

"He's a one-person horse," Ian agreed.

Cindy nodded, but for just a moment she stood very still, hardly aware of the shouts and bustle of the colorful crowd surrounding her. A quick stab of grief pierced her heart as she remembered another one-person horse—Storm's Ransom, Whitebrook's prize sprinter, who had died just two months ago.

After Storm's early death Cindy had grieved for the sweet, beautiful gray colt until she was almost sick. She knew she wasn't really over it yet. *At least Champion keeps me busy*, she thought.

"Let's go to the stands and watch the post parade," Ian suggested.

"Okay." Cindy took a deep breath and tried to clear away her thoughts of the past. Today was a big day for Champion, and she wanted to give the race her full attention. As she followed her dad and Mike through the throngs of people spending the pleasant summer day at the races, she wondered how Champion would do. Several of the top two-year-olds in the country were entered in the Bashford Manor, a grade-three stakes.

Champion will have to run well to win, she thought. The victory would be an important one. The Bashford Manor was the first of four races called the Kentucky Thoroughbred Development Fund Bonus Series. The races would be run over the summer and fall at the different Kentucky tracks: the Bashford at Churchill Downs, the Juvenile Stakes at Ellis Park, the Kentucky Cup Juvenile Stakes at Turfway Park, and the Breeders' Futurity at Keeneland. Any horse that won all four races would get a bonus. If Champion did well today, Ian and Mike planned to run him in the entire series.

In the stands Cindy's adoptive mother, Beth McLean, was waiting with Christina, Ashleigh's year-and-a-half-old daughter, and Kevin, Cindy's brother, who had just turned a year old.

"Hi, Cindy," Beth said, handing red-haired Kevin to Ian. "Did you get Champion all set?"

"We think so." Cindy picked up her binoculars and studied the field. Champion was sidestepping and pulling at the reins, but Ashleigh wasn't having much trouble controlling him. She was keeping him well away from the other horses.

Champion balked, digging in his heels, as the attendants tried to lead him into the gate. "Come on, Champion," Mike muttered.

Cindy bit her lip. Nothing Champion had done so far today had ruined his chances yet, but his behavior meant that he was in a bad mood. Usually it took her a full workout with him to get him out of a mood like that. That meant he might act up the entire race.

With five attendants pushing and pulling, Champion finally loaded in the gate.

"It's good he's drawn the three position," Samantha remarked. "Ashleigh can take him straight to the front."

"I bet she'll have to," Cindy murmured. Champion hated to be behind other horses. When Cindy exercise-rode him in the mornings, she tried to avoid certain other colts entirely. Champion had very distinct likes and dislikes about people and horses. He wasn't above showing it sometimes with a good nip.

"Champion's rearing in the starting gate!" Samantha cried.

"Hold him steady, Ashleigh," Mike said.

"She's trying!" Cindy could hardly stand to watch. The starting gate was a dangerous place. If Champion reared and lost his balance in the narrow space of the stall, Ashleigh could be crushed against the side. If she fell, she could be trampled under the colt's hooves.

To Cindy's immense relief, Champion's head bobbed down in the gate. The next second the doors flipped open.

"And they're off!" the announcer called.

"I hope Ashleigh's balanced in the saddle!" Samantha squeezed her hands anxiously.

"She looks okay. There goes Champion to the front!" Mike shouted.

The horses flew across the backstretch. From there, Cindy could hear only a distant pounding of hooves, as if the thick, humid summer air were trapping the sound. She quickly adjusted her binoculars. "Syncope's already pressing Champion," she said. The gray Florida-bred colt slowly gained on Champion until the two horses were running neck and neck.

"No surprise," Mike said. "Syncope's got a lot of early speed."

Suddenly Champion bore out sharply instead of following the inside rail. "What's he doing?" Cindy cried in alarm.

"He's going after the other colt!" Mike said in disbelief.

"Ashleigh's got to straighten him out," Cindy said. She jumped up, clenching and unclenching her hands. If Champion and Syncope started fighting at that speed, they could knock each other off balance and fall. And the other four horses in the field were bearing down on the front-runners. They could fall, too, and cause a lot of injury.

Cindy wanted to close her eyes, but she forced herself to watch. *No matter what happens, Champion's my colt,* she thought.

Ashleigh was pulling Champion's head to the inside, but Cindy could see that the colt's attention was still fixed on Syncope.

"Last Gulch is making his move to the inside!" the announcer called suddenly. "He's taken the lead!"

Cindy saw that just enough space had opened up on the rail for Last Gulch, a chestnut colt known to be a closer, to slip through going into the turn. "Don't let him do it, Champion!" she cried. Champion was so busy watching Syncope, he didn't seem to see that he was only tied for second place! Last Gulch drew off by a length, then two lengths. Cindy ground her teeth in frustration.

"Champion's not in good position for a six-furlong race." Ian groaned. "Come on, Champion. Put your heart into it!"

Suddenly Champion saw the colt ahead of him. With a bound he switched leads going into the stretch and pounded after his rival.

"That's the way!" Cindy called. *For the first time in the race Champion and Ashleigh seem in complete agreement about what to do,* Cindy noted with relief.

"I wish Champion had listened to Ashleigh earlier," Samantha yelled over the excited cheers of the crowd. "I don't think he can make up enough ground before the wire!"

Don't count him out yet! Now Cindy could clearly see the field as they passed in front of the stands, heading for home. Champion was in high gear, his powerful, slender legs churning up the soft dirt of the track. Cindy could almost feel how hard the colt was driving as he reached for ground. Slowly he pulled even with Last Gulch's flank, and then the two colts were head-to-head.

"Champion's got it!" Cindy shouted.

"Not quite!" Samantha cried as Last Gulch's nose bobbed in front.

Champion's ears swept back. *Is he going to bite Gulch?* Cindy wondered frantically.

Instead Champion poured on a burst of pure speed! Cindy could hardly breathe as the colt roared ahead, a surging chocolate streak.

"Wonder's Champion takes it by a nose," the announcer called.

"Whew!" Cindy dropped back into her seat, fanning her face. "Wasn't that great?" she asked, turning excitedly to Samantha.

"It sure was," Samantha agreed. "And luckily none of us had a heart attack!"

"Let's get down to the winner's circle," Cindy said, leading the way out of the stands.

Ashleigh was bringing Champion back to the gap at a slow gallop. The colt was moving easily but still fighting for rein. White flecks of sweat dotted his dark brown coat.

"That was a wild ride." Ashleigh dismounted and took off her helmet, shaking out her hair.

"You look exhausted!" Mike said with concern.

"But we won!" Ashleigh grinned at Cindy. She lifted off Champion's saddle to weigh in.

"That's right." Cindy hugged the colt. *He acted up, but the important thing is that he was first under the wire,* she thought. "Good job, big guy!" she congratulated him.

Champion bent his elegant head to sniff her hair. After a few moments his small, well-shaped ears tipped back, and he seemed to relax.

Ashleigh walked over and stood next to Champion for the winning photo. Cindy and the rest of the Whitebrook group gathered close to get in the picture.

"Don't take long, you guys," Ashleigh warned the photographers. "Champion isn't going to stand still for more than another second."

Cindy rubbed the colt's neck to distract him. "I'm sure you'll do even better in your next race," she said. "You're going to be standing in a lot of winner's circles, boy."

Champion tossed his head and stared boldly into the cameras, as if he thought so, too.

2

"CINDY, MAX IS ON THE PHONE!" BETH CALLED UP THE stairs the next morning.

"I'll get it up here." Cindy hurried from her room to pick up the hall phone. Max Smith, the son of Whitebrook's vet, would be in ninth grade with Cindy in the fall. He was one of Cindy's best friends. "Hi, Max, what's up?" she said.

"I just got back from helping my mom with a difficult foaling," Max replied. "The new colt's fine now—it was just turned wrong."

"I'm glad he's okay. Do you want to come over here and play with our foals?" Cindy asked. Eleven new foals had been born at Whitebrook that year. Cindy loved watching the small horses frolic in the paddock.

"Sure," Max said. "I'll ask my mom if I can come—

hold on." He returned and said, "She said yes. She'll bring me over in a few minutes."

"See you then." Cindy hung up the phone and returned to her room. She sat on her bed, deep in thought.

I spend a lot more time inside than I used to before Storm died, she thought. Cindy reached to touch Storm's special blue-and-white saddlecloth, which hung on her wall. The saddlecloth had been a Christmas present from Cindy's family, and Storm had worn it in his last races. Cindy sighed as she pressed her cheek to the soft material.

"I guess I'm getting over him a little," she murmured. For the first days after Storm's death she had barely been able to drag herself out of bed. But now Cindy helped to feed, groom, and muck out stalls every morning the way she always had. She also exercise-rode Champion. Sometimes, though, she wasn't sure if her concentration was as good as it had been when Storm was alive.

The equine infectious anemia epidemic that had taken Storm's life had died down quickly in Kentucky. No new cases had been reported in the past two months. Cindy knew it was time to move on with her life, but some days she found it very hard.

Champion had returned home from Churchill Downs yesterday, right after his victory in the Bashford, and Cindy had walked him that morning on Whitebrook's mile-long training track. Champion had come out of the race fine despite his effort. Wonder's other offspring had suffered health problems, but Cindy had a hunch that Champion was the strongest of them.

He'll win his races, she assured herself. *Maybe Champion will deserve a special saddlecloth soon, too.*

Cindy got up and hurried down the stairs into the kitchen. Samantha was sitting at the table, reading a trade horse magazine. "Where are you off to?" she asked.

"The paddocks and the training barn. Max and I are going to look at the horses and probably ride." Cindy grabbed a red apple out of the refrigerator and took a bite.

"Mr. Wonderful is racing in the Hollywood Gold Cup today," Samantha said. "We want to watch it on TV—don't stay out too late or you'll miss it."

"I definitely won't miss it," Cindy said. She hadn't forgotten that Mr. Wonderful, Wonder's four-year-old son and Champion's half-brother, was running at Hollywood Park in the second race in the MGM Classic Crown series. Mr. Wonderful had already won the Santa Anita Handicap, the first race in the series, after missing the Triple Crown races last year due to injury.

Cindy opened the door to her family's cottage and walked slowly to the front paddock, where the foals

15

and their dams were grazing. The day was already very warm, and a soft haze had settled over the hills. Today the big red-painted training barn and the smaller mares' and stallions' barns seemed almost to melt against the pale blue sky.

Cindy glanced back at her family's white cottage, where she had lived for three years since the McLeans adopted her, and at Ashleigh and Mike's rambling, two-hundred-year-old farmhouse. Ahead were acres of white-fenced paddocks, filled with the lively foals and their dams; the stallions; and the muscular, sleek horses in training. As always, Cindy's heart lifted at the beauty of the farm. *I couldn't love living here more,* she thought.

Max was walking up the driveway. "Hi, Cindy," he called.

"Hi." Cindy noticed that Max's dark hair had lighter streaks from being in the sun as he went on rounds with his mother. His eyes shone bright green against his tan face.

Both Cindy and Max jumped at a sharp crack in the front paddock and the quick thunder of hooves. She spun around. The group of foals were flying across the paddock. "What was that?" she asked Max, breaking into a run.

"It sounded like one of the horses kicked the fence," Max called after her.

Please don't let it be Honor Bright, Cindy prayed as

she quickly opened the gate. The exquisite, spirited bay daughter of Townsend Princess was Cindy's special favorite of this year's foal crop. If Honor had kicked the board fence and injured her leg, her career as a racehorse could have ended in that split second.

"It was Hero's Welcome," Max said, pointing to a light gray mare standing in front of the fence.

The mare's tail was whisking rapidly over her smooth coat. "I think a fly was bothering Hero, and that's why she kicked out," Cindy said. She pushed the mare away from the fence and gently lifted her leg. "It seems fine," she said with relief.

"Look around—you've got company." Max laughed.

Cindy turned. While she had been examining Hero's leg, the entire group of foals had quietly approached Cindy from behind. Now she was surrounded by nearly a dozen small, inquisitive black, brown, and gray faces, with all different shapes of stars, blazes, and snips. Cindy had to laugh at the young horses' curious expressions.

"Honor!" she called, stretching out her hand. Honor Bright wasn't the biggest foal in the crop, but she had a strong personality and was the dominant foal, even over the colts.

The perfect little bay filly whickered and pushed to the front of the pack to touch Cindy's fingertips with her soft muzzle. Only six weeks old, Honor Bright was already the fastest foal at Whitebrook. She had a star and Wonder's trademark snip at the end of her nose.

Townsend Princess glanced around to see where her foal was, then went back to grazing the abundant grass. Cindy was a familiar visitor to the paddock, and the mare trusted her with her baby.

"Nine fillies, but only two colts, were born at Whitebrook this year," Cindy said to Max. The ten other foals crowded around, bumping her hands as they begged for attention. The mares were too busy cropping the luxuriant green grass to take much notice of Max and Cindy.

"That's pretty unusual," Max said, patting Fleet Goddess's stocky black filly, Fleet Street. Fleet Goddess was one of Ashleigh's former race mares.

"Yeah. I think it means at least one of the fillies will be really special." Honor Bright had stepped away, and Cindy looked her over carefully. Honor wasn't only spunky, she was perfectly conformed, Cindy thought. Her deep chest and correct legs already seemed to foretell speed and stamina at the track.

"It's almost like Honor got a turn being patted, and now she's letting the other foals get close to us," Max remarked. "That was nice of her."

"That's how she got her name," Cindy said. "One day Lucky Chance, Shining's filly"—Cindy pointed to a slender black filly—"nipped Honor. Honor chased Lucky and pinned her in a corner. But then she let her go. Samantha was watching and called it 'victory with honor.' That's when I got the idea of calling her Honor Bright."

"Cool name," Max remarked.

"It suits her—not just her honor is bright," Cindy said fondly. "So is the rest of her." She couldn't take her eyes off the young foal. Honor Bright was frisking across the thick grass. The filly was a beautiful bright bay, with a black mane, tail, and stockings. "Champion is her uncle," Cindy added. "He was the most impressive foal in his crop, too."

"Do you want to go see him?" Max asked. "He's right over there." Max pointed to one of the smaller paddocks to their left.

"Yeah, he hates to be left out." Cindy had already noticed that Champion was watching them, tossing his head impatiently and pushing against the boards of the fence.

"What's next for him?" Max asked as they walked to Champion's paddock. Looking back over her shoulder, Cindy saw that the other foals were following Honor, running their hearts out in a play race.

"Probably Champion won't race until the Juvenile Stakes at Ellis Park in September," Cindy said. "He's only two—Mike and my dad don't want to overrace him."

Cindy frowned a little. She knew that Champion's young age wasn't the only reason his trainers didn't want to race him for a while. Despite Champion's victory yesterday Ashleigh, Ian, and Mike weren't completely satisfied with the colt's performance.

"He's got an attitude problem," Ashleigh had said in the barn after the race. "I don't want to take away from his victory—it was stunning. But in his next race Champion's got to go another furlong, and he only won the Bashford and his maiden race by a nose. We have to get to the root of his training problem, whatever it is."

I wonder what's gotten into Champion? Cindy thought. *His training was going so well for a while this year. Everybody thought that he'd finally grown up and knew what to do.*

"There's the Champion," Max said, patting Champion's blaze.

The big colt eyed him, then threw up his head with a snort. He turned to Cindy and pricked his ears.

"Oh, you're still my big baby." Cindy scratched Champion's ears and rubbed his dark brown neck. The colt bent his head, eating up her caresses.

"He sure does like you," Max said.

"I like him, too." Cindy smiled. She glanced up as a cool breeze fluttered her hair. Purple and gray thunderclouds were building rapidly in the west. "I'd better go weed the flowers on Storm's grave before it rains and I get soaked," she said.

"You still miss him, don't you?" Max said sympathetically.

"Yes." Cindy sighed. "Storm was the opposite of Champion. He was so gentle. I mean, this morning one of the newspapers reviewing Champion's last race called him the most dangerous horse they'd ever seen, even though he won."

"He may snap out of it," Max said.

"Probably," Cindy agreed. "If we can figure out why he acts the way he does."

"Just keep thinking about it," Max advised.

Cindy and Max stayed with Champion for a little longer, then she and Max went back to the foals' paddock to play with Honor Bright and the others. Cindy kept an eye on the sky the whole time. *I really want to get out to Storm's grave before it rains, but I don't want Max to come with me*, she thought. Somehow going to see her beloved horse was too personal to share.

"I should go home and help my mom with our horses," Max said finally, giving Fleet Street a last rub. "Maybe tomorrow we can go swimming."

Cindy nodded. "I'll call Heather," she said. Heather Gilbert, who was also going into ninth grade, was Cindy's other best friend.

Max headed up to the McLeans' cottage to call his mom. Cindy started to walk along the lane to the meadow but stopped at the sound of a loud whinny. Looking back, she saw that Champion was at the gate, eagerly hanging his head over the top board.

21

"Do you want to go with me to see Storm's grave?" Cindy asked with a smile.

That spring, when Champion had been acting up in training, Ashleigh had suggested that Cindy spend as much time as possible with the colt. Cindy had followed her suggestion. Soon she noticed that Champion had become much more responsive to her voice. In the beginning of the year that had seemed to help when she exercised him on the training track.

Cindy frowned slightly. She still had no idea why Champion had started acting up again. Sometimes his workouts were as erratic as his performances on the track.

Turning his head sideways, Champion thrust his muzzle through the boards of the gate. Cindy laughed. "I'll take that as a yes," she said. She quickly haltered him and opened the gate.

As Cindy and Champion passed the foals' paddock she saw that all the young horses except Honor Bright were lying flat on their sides next to their mothers, sleeping. But Honor was awake and restlessly pacing the fence line. The small bay filly's bright eyes were fixed on Cindy.

"I know—you'd like to come. I'll take you somewhere soon," Cindy promised. "Maybe just around the paddock, since you can't be away from your mom yet."

Champion pulled hard on the lead. He seemed to

be saying that he didn't want to share Cindy's company. "Okay, we're going, Champion," Cindy said. "Just be patient for once."

Storm had been buried in a big meadow, dotted with flowers, at the foot of a small hill. Sadness filled Cindy's heart as she and Champion approached the lovely spot.

"Hi, Storm," she said softly, kneeling by the grave. She reached to touch the vibrant, bright orange petals of a tiger lily.

Champion placidly cropped grass as Cindy carefully tended the warm-colored, sweet-smelling flowers. He was used to Cindy's daily routine with Storm.

At last she sat back on her heels, satisfied with the way the grave looked. "You deserve a pretty place to be, Storm," she whispered. "You were so beautiful." Cindy brushed away her tears.

She'd had so many dreams for Storm. Last fall and winter he had run his heart out. He had run so well, she had thought there wasn't any sprint he couldn't win. Now all those dreams were shattered. Cindy dropped her head, overcome with grief.

A sharp tug on the lead line reminded Cindy she wasn't alone. Champion was looking at her intently. Cindy sighed. *He's bored,* she thought. *Probably I should walk him or work with him somehow. But I want to stay here just a little longer.* Cindy looked back at the grave.

"What should I do about Champion, Storm?" she asked. "How can I make him behave the way you did?"

The meadow was silent and peaceful. Cindy shook her head. *I guess I'll have to figure that one out for myself*, she realized.

Champion hauled on the lead line, almost pulling Cindy over. "Oh, stop it. Okay, let's go." Cindy got up and brushed off her jeans. She smiled as Champion eagerly pushed her from behind, as if to say, Now you've got the right idea—finally!

After they had walked a few steps Cindy stopped and looked back. Storm's grave looked so peaceful under the warm, bright sun. "I know I'll never forget you, Storm," she said quietly. "I don't think any other horse can really take your place."

"It's Ashleigh!" Cindy said that night after dinner, cupping her hand over the cordless phone. Cindy and her family had just finished watching Mr. Wonderful take second in the Hollywood Gold Cup Handicap. He had lost by two lengths to a Kentucky-bred colt from a neighboring farm. "How is Mr. Wonderful?" Cindy asked Ashleigh anxiously. From what Cindy had seen on TV, it wasn't clear to her why Mr. Wonderful had lost.

Ashleigh hesitated. "He faded," she said finally.

"I don't believe it!" Cindy was stunned. Mr.

Wonderful had done magnificently in his previous races that year. He had won the Donn Handicap at Gulfstream Park in Florida and the Santa Anita Handicap in California, both grade-one races.

"I know, I almost don't believe it, either," Ashleigh said. "But as Mr. Wonderful's jockey, I could tell that he just didn't have what it takes. We think he came out of the race okay, though."

"That's good," Cindy said. She tried to think what she could say to comfort Ashleigh. Ashleigh sounded so disappointed. "Maybe he'll come back in time for the Pacific Classic." Until today's loss Mr. Wonderful had been entered in the grade-one race at Del Mar in California. The Santa Anita Handicap, the Hollywood Gold Cup, and the Pacific Classic races made up the MGM bonus series. Until Mr. Wonderful's defeat in the Gold Cup today, Cindy knew he had been favored to win all three races.

"We'll see about running him again this summer." Ashleigh sighed. "I'm trying to be a good sport about our loss today, but I had hoped so much that Mr. Wonderful would sweep the MGM series. Maybe I'm wrong, but I think Mr. Wonderful's racing career may be over."

"You're kidding," Cindy gasped. She prayed that wasn't true.

"Hey, I should let you go," Ashleigh said. "We'll

talk about all this when I get home day after tomorrow. Say hi to everybody."

"I will." Cindy returned to her seat at the kitchen table. Ian was at the track with Mr. Wonderful, but Beth, Samantha, and Kevin were finishing dessert.

"So what does Ashleigh think happened?" Samantha asked, setting down her dessert spoon.

"She's not sure. Mr. Wonderful faded, but he doesn't seem to be injured or sick." Cindy stared at her banana split, a rich concoction of vanilla, strawberries, chocolate ice cream, and thick whipped cream, without really seeing it.

"Well, at least Mr. Wonderful seems to be okay," Beth said gently.

"I know," Cindy agreed. "That's the important thing." After Storm's death, she was sure of it.

3

ON THE FOURTH OF JULY, CINDY RODE CHAMPION OUT TO the training track for his first workout since the Bashford. The giant red ball of the early morning sun was slowly rising on the horizon. The summer morning was cool and still, with birds chirping in the trees.

The dark chestnut colt danced along the path, tossing his head and snorting. "You know where we're going, don't you?" Cindy asked, leaning forward to pat his glossy neck. "Let's show them something good today, Champion. You won your last race, but I'm not sure everyone is completely happy with you anyway."

Champion looked at her backward, his prominent dark eyes glinting. He was definitely ready for action. *Now if only he wants to run and not pull tricks,* Cindy thought. She knew how dangerous the colt could be when he was in a bad mood. Champion had dumped her a couple of times, once almost breaking her arm. She wasn't eager to repeat the experience.

Samantha and Ashleigh were already out on the track, riding Limitless Time and Freedom's Ring. Limitless Time, the two-year-old son of Fleet Goddess, was showing great progress in his workouts, and Cindy knew that her dad and Mike planned to race him in the fall at Churchill Downs or Keeneland. Freedom's Ring, a well-made black colt bought at the September Keeneland selected yearling sale, easily matched strides with Limitless Time.

Ashleigh and Samantha were keeping the horses toward the center of the track at a slow gallop. The horses rose and fell at the controlled pace, their silhouettes dark against the brilliant orange-and-red early morning sky.

Cindy sighed with admiration. She knew that everyone at Whitebrook thought she rode Champion very well, and before that Cindy had been instrumental in training March to Glory, who had set a world record in the Breeders' Cup Classic last year. *But I wonder if I'll ever be as perfect a rider as Ashleigh or Samantha*, she thought.

Mike and Ian stood at the rail, intently watching the two young horses. "Hi," Cindy said. "How are they doing?"

"Not bad." Ian shaded his eyes from the sun. "Freedom seems to be maturing much slower than Champion or Limitless, though. I don't think he'll race as a two-year-old. We'll see this fall."

Cindy glanced down at Champion. The colt was fidgeting and hauling at the reins, encouraging her to take him out on the track. *You're bad sometimes, Champion, but nobody has any doubt that you're ready to race*, she thought with a smile.

"Cindy, wait until Ashleigh gets here," Mike said. "She wants to talk to you before you take Champion out."

"Okay." Ian was Champion's official trainer, but as the colt's jockey Ashleigh always had a lot of input on his training. "Just take it easy, Champion."

The colt rolled an eye around at her. But he stood very still, watching alertly as Ashleigh brought Freedom's Ring back around to the gap at a brisk trot.

"Let's get Champion out there, Cindy," Ashleigh said, quickly dismounting and handing Freedom's reins to Mike. "We've got a lot to work on with him before the Juvenile Stakes. I knew that right away after his performance in the Bashford."

"So did I," Ian said ruefully. "The track officials made it clear to me they thought so, too."

"What do you mean?" Cindy frowned.

"Champion caused so much trouble at the track—

in the walking ring, at the gate, and in the race itself," Ashleigh said. "Next time he acts like that, the officials will almost certainly make us scratch him from the race. Champion did win the Bashford impressively, and he didn't hurt another horse or jockey—this time. But the officials at Ellis Park will be watching him closely in the Juvenile Stakes."

Cindy bit her lip. *How can Ashleigh and I get through to Champion so that he doesn't act like that?* she wondered. She remembered again how well the colt had done earlier in the spring in his gate training and some of his gallops. "Why is he doing this now?" she asked.

"I don't know." Ashleigh ran a hand through her thick dark hair. "I thought we had gotten him through the worst of his shenanigans last spring. He seemed to have grown up, and all that time you've spent with him after his workouts seemed to have helped."

Cindy felt a stab of guilt. For the past two months she had spent a lot of time with Champion in the afternoons—but usually they only went to visit Storm. Cindy wasn't sure if that really counted as quality time with Champion. *But maybe it does*, she thought. "What do you want him to do now?" she asked.

"Give him a very thorough warm-up," Ashleigh said. "Trot him once around, then a slow gallop. I don't want you to work him today unless you can keep him under control."

It's back to square one, Cindy realized as she touched up the colt with her heels, heading counter-clockwise around the oval. "Champion, it's awful that nobody trusts you anymore," she said. "What happened to you this spring and summer? Did you just get tired of being good?"

Champion frisked along at the trot, his gait strong and floating. His ears flicked back, listening to her voice. He seemed content to mind for the moment.

"I guess you were never very obedient in the first place," Cindy said with a smile. "But you have a lot of talent, Champion. And I know you like to win. You just have to put those two things together."

The sun had lifted in the sky, and its beams tinted the thick grass of the surrounding paddocks a warm yellow. Champion's smooth, deep brown coat twinkled in the strong light, the color of a rich chocolate bar. Impulsively Cindy leaned forward to hug him. No matter how badly he behaved, she loved the spirited colt.

As they passed the gap for the first time Cindy leaned forward in the small exercise saddle, asking Champion for a gallop. With no hesitation he broke into the faster gait.

"That's the way," Cindy encouraged. As always she marveled at the colt's quick, effortless strides. In three years of exercise riding at Whitebrook, Cindy had ridden a lot of fast horses, but she had always felt there was something special about Champion. *When you're riding him, you don't really know that he's fast,* she thought. *He makes it seem so easy.*

The breeze was cool and fresh at this speed. Cindy pushed her hair out of her eyes with one hand, focusing on the track ahead. In no time they had lapped the track, and Cindy pulled back on the reins, asking the colt to slow at the gap.

Champion obeyed perfectly, instantly breaking into a quick trot. "What a good boy!" Cindy praised, patting his neck.

Ashleigh consulted with Ian for a few moments. "Let's work Champion three furlongs, Cindy," she called. "Start at the three-eighths pole."

"Okay!" *We did well—Champion's behaving today!* she thought. Cindy was eager to be off again. When Champion was in a good mood like this, he treated her to the rides of her life.

She could tell that the big colt shared her enthusiasm. Champion plunged into a gallop at her signals, kicking up the fine dirt of the track. Cindy leaned into the motion of the fast gait. As she enjoyed the rhythmic beat of his hooves Cindy forgot how contentious the colt could be. She only wanted to ride on like this forever.

In no time the three-eighths pole flashed by. "Go!" Cindy cried, moving even farther over the colt's withers.

Suddenly Cindy felt Champion kick in. The

ground whipped by in a blur as the colt's even strides became longer.

"Great, Champion," Cindy cried. "That's the way!"

Then, to her amazement, the colt found another gear. They had been going unbelievably fast before, but now they were flying!

Should I try to rate him? Cindy wondered, her cheeks flushed with exhilaration. *I never knew a horse could do this!* Cindy worried that she might do the wrong thing, but nothing could take away from the rush she felt. In seconds they raced by the gap. Cindy let the colt gallop out another quarter, then turned him. Laughing with joy, she pulled Champion up at the gap.

"How fast?" she asked breathlessly.

"Want to guess?" Ashleigh asked with a smile.

Cindy thought back to her sensation of flying and tried to estimate how that translated into real time. "Thirty-six seconds," she said finally.

"Thirty-five." Ashleigh held up the stopwatch. "And he wasn't even trying."

"I think we've got something here," Ian said.

"I know we do!" Cindy swung her leg over the saddle to dismount just as Champion skittered sideways. Cindy wobbled as she jumped off and barely kept her balance. "You had to do that, didn't you?" she asked.

The colt dropped his head to look at her. He

seemed to be teasing as he dodged the warning finger she shook at him.

I think you'll do fine in your next race, Cindy thought as she gathered Champion's reins to take him back to the barn. *You're just mischievous. I know you'll want to run that fast again. You enjoyed it as much as I did.*

At dusk Cindy and Samantha walked to the car to join the rest of their family for an evening of Fourth of July fireworks. Cindy could already hear the distant pop of a few early fireworks and see the soft explosion of colored light against the dark clouds.

"Look at Champion go!" Samantha said, laughing.

Champion was roaring around one of the front paddocks, spooked from the fireworks. Len, the stable manager, stood at the paddock gate, patiently waiting for the colt to stand still so that he could bring him in for the night.

Cindy grinned, admiring Champion's quick turn at the back of the paddock. The colt darted back for the gate at a fast gallop. "I think Len's going to have his hands full catching him," she said.

"Are Heather and Mandy coming with us?" Beth asked as Cindy opened the car door.

"No—we'll meet them over there. Max is coming, too." Cindy climbed into the backseat with Samantha and Kevin, stepping over Kevin's car seat. "You're such a cutie, Kevin," she said, squeezing the baby's small hand. With his red hair and green eyes, he looked like a miniature Samantha, Cindy thought. Kevin bounced in the seat and smiled.

"Everybody's raring to go," Samantha said with a laugh.

A large crowd had already gathered at the field outside Lexington where the fireworks display would be held. People had brought picnic baskets and were sitting on the tailgates of trucks or on blankets spread beside their cars.

"I have no idea how I'm going to find my friends." Cindy glanced around at the milling throng.

"Maybe they'll find you," Beth said, setting a picnic basket on the ground. "Do you want a cold drink?"

"Sure." Cindy took the soda Beth offered her, flipped the tab, and took a long, cool swig. The evening was muggy, with a close, thick feel, and in the distance heat lightning lit up the sky.

"It's almost time for the fireworks," Samantha said. "I wonder where Tor is?" Tor Nelson, Samantha's longtime boyfriend, ran a jumping stable with his father in Lexington.

"Here he comes." Cindy pointed. "And Heather, Mandy, and Max are with him," she added with relief.

"Hi, you guys," Tor said. Samantha's tall, blond boyfriend bent over to kiss her cheek.

"How did you find everybody?" Cindy asked, waving hello to her friends.

"I bumped into Heather and Max at the gate," Tor said. "Mandy had a jumping lesson, so she just came over with me in the truck. But I don't think the lesson has stopped—she's still been bugging me with questions!"

Everybody laughed. Ten-year-old Mandy's dedication to jumping was legendary among her friends.

"Oh, well," Mandy said, her dark eyes twinkling. "I just want to get a jump on the competition, you know."

"There go the fireworks!" Heather said, her blond ponytail bouncing. Heather was almost as dedicated to horses as Cindy was. She also took jumping lessons at Tor's stable.

"Everybody take a seat," Ian urged, unfolding the striped lawn chairs they had brought from home. "Let's enjoy this."

Cindy plopped in a chair and tilted her head to look up at the sky. Red, white, and blue fireworks raced across the black night in burst after burst of color. "Wow, they're gorgeous!" she said.

"They sure are," Max agreed, settling into a chair next to hers.

Those fireworks explode just like a fast closer at the end of a horserace, Cindy thought, resting her head against the back of her chair. She'd been up since five working with the horses, and she was so sleepy now, the fireworks seemed like a dream. *Champion could be a really fast closer since he seems to have two higher gears—one when he changes leads and another when he gets right near the wire.*

Heather and Mandy were laughing at something Samantha had said. Max didn't join in or even seem to notice. Cindy looked over at him. She realized he'd been quiet all evening. "Is something wrong?" she asked.

"No." Max hesitated, looking at his hands. "I guess I'm just thinking about how I have to spend most of the summer in Seattle with my dad. I mean, I'm always glad to see him, but I'd rather stay here with my mom, you, and the horses."

Cindy nodded. She knew she would feel the same way. "But you'll be back for school right after Labor Day," she said. "We'll have fun then. And I bet I'll have a lot to show you with Champion. I think maybe I can trust him now—his workouts should be smooth sailing, and so should the Juvenile Stakes."

4

"Isn't summer great?" Cindy said to Heather a week later as she reined in Glory on the trail behind Whitebrook. The big gray stallion tossed his head and walked spiritedly down the path under the heavy, rustling leaves of the trees.

Cindy loved summers at Whitebrook. The days seem to stretch forward endlessly, full of horses, riding, and hot sunshine.

She dropped her head and rested her cheek against Glory's warm, satin neck. Glory looked backward at her, his gaze fond and contented. "You haven't changed much since the days when you were on the track," she said. "You were always a great guy. I hope your foals are that way, too." Glory had been bred for the first time that year, and his first foals were due the next winter.

"Maybe he'll have little Glorys that are just as great as he was on the track," Heather said, pulling up Chips, the horse she was riding, beside Glory. The gentle Appaloosa leaned forward, tugging at the reins to reach the bright green foliage. Heather let him eat a bite.

"I sure hope so." Cindy looked thoughtful. "But breeding's a tricky thing. I mean, Glory was the first outstanding offspring of his sire and dam and even of his grandsire, Just Victory. But all Wonder's offspring have been incredible."

"They sure have," Heather agreed.

"That's why everyone is so interested in Champion." Cindy said, shifting in the saddle and narrowing her eyes. "What if he's the next Wonder's Pride?" Wonder's first son had won the Kentucky Derby and the Belmont Stakes and was now at stud at Whitebrook. "Or Champion could be even better than Pride," Cindy added. Sometimes she just had a feeling about Champion—that he was really going to be something.

"Do you think he could be?" Heather asked seriously.

"I don't know." Cindy let Glory's reins out a notch. The stallion obediently moved out at a walk, his silken tail swishing. "Champion's only run in two races, and his performance was inconsistent," she called over her shoulder. "It's hard to tell much from that—except that he can be pretty wild."

"At least he didn't get hurt," Heather remarked, trotting Chips to catch up with Glory.

"No. I didn't expect him to," Cindy said thoughtfully. "I mean, accidents on the track can always happen, but Wonder and Pride raced until they were four, and Mr. Wonderful is still going strong at four."

"It's so exciting that Mr. Wonderful is going to race in the Pacific Classic after all," Heather said.

"Yeah, I know." Ashleigh had called that morning from the Del Mar track with the good news, and Cindy had immediately told Heather. Mr. Wonderful had been moved to Del Mar, where Ashleigh had said the colt was training well.

"Well, I hope he wins," Heather said.

Cindy frowned slightly. "He should. The vet checked him over completely after he lost the Hollywood Gold Cup. She couldn't find anything wrong."

"So what does Ashleigh think happened?" Heather asked.

"She says we may never know." Cindy asked Glory for a trot, and the stallion lightly quickened his pace. "After Mr. Wonderful runs in the Pacific Classic, she said maybe we would see a pattern. But she hopes not, because that would mean he'd lose again."

"Champion's got a pattern of winning," Heather said, sounding breathless as she trotted Chips after

Glory. Chips had to take almost two strides for every one stride of Glory's.

"Yeah, but winning two races as a two-year-old doesn't mean Champion will train on," Cindy answered. "I hope it does, but after the way he acted in the Bashford, I'm worried about him."

"Do you think he'll cause trouble in his next race?" Heather asked.

"I hope not." Glory's ears were tipped back, awaiting Cindy's instructions. Cindy smiled. "Hey, Glory boy," she whispered fondly. Glory looked back again at her appreciatively. *When Champion looks at me, I can tell he likes me, too, but something else is always there, deep down,* Cindy thought. *Champion sure loves to make trouble!* "Champion really has to be on his best behavior in his next race, the Juvenile Stakes," she added. "If he isn't, the track officials will make us scratch him."

"So what are you going to do to make him behave better?" Heather looked puzzled.

"I'm not sure. Sometimes he behaves perfectly, but I don't know why. He did that fantastic work last week, just flying along, and he hardly had to make an effort. The last horse I rode who ran like that was Glory." Cindy reached back to pat the stallion behind the saddle. "But I don't know how to make Champion run like that when I want," she added. "His last two works were bad again." Cindy didn't

41

want to dwell on just how bad. The colt had been in one of his worst moods both times, and he had acted just as out of control as he had been in the Bashford.

"Maybe you just have to hope for the best with him," Heather said.

"Yeah, but that's not good enough. He won't win a lot of races that way." Cindy sighed. "I love him, and I think he could be a great racehorse. I just wish I knew what makes him tick. He's so smart, I know he's thinking a lot. But I don't always know *what* he's thinking."

Heather pointed to a lush patch of grass illuminated by slanting sunlight through the trees. "Do you want to have our picnic here?"

"Sure." Cindy quickly dismounted and haltered Glory. She tied him in the shade of a large oak.

Heather tied Chips nearby. "So what's for lunch?" she asked with a laugh. "You made it."

"That's why it's leftover pizza from dinner last night. Beth didn't have time to help me make lunch before she left for work this morning," Cindy said. She unwrapped a foil-covered slice of pizza and bit into spicy pepperoni. She leaned back against a tree, studying Glory. The graceful stallion stood quietly, flicking his sides with his tail. "Glory's so much like his grandsire," she said.

"Didn't you say Champion is like his sire?" Heather asked.

Cindy nodded. "Townsend Victor was a handful. There's a story about how he got to be that way, though. Townsend Victor was a Townsend Acres horse until he had to be destroyed a month ago when he went through a fence."

Ashleigh's Wonder had been bred and born at Townsend Acres, a huge Thoroughbred training and breeding farm, when Ashleigh's parents had worked there as breeding managers. After Ashleigh had helped to train Wonder into a champion, Clay Townsend, the owner of the farm, had given Ashleigh a half interest in Wonder and all her offspring. For a long time the arrangement had caused strife between the two farms as each battled to keep Wonder and her offspring on their premises. Ashleigh had to trade the Townsends a half interest in Glory to keep Champion in training at Whitebrook.

Luckily, for a long time now the Townsends hadn't interfered in Mr. Wonderful's or Champion's training, Cindy thought with relief. Usually a member of the family showed up for the bigger races, but Cindy had heard that Clay Townsend was busy expanding his business interests abroad. Brad Townsend, the owner's son and a particular enemy of Ashleigh, had kept his distance for the past year or so.

Maybe he actually thinks Ashleigh knows what she's doing with the horses, Cindy said to herself. *We don't need his help!*

Heather made a face. "So the Townsends didn't treat Townsend Victor well? I mean, even before he went through the fence?"

"That's what Hank thinks," Cindy said, referring to the head groom at Townsend Acres. "He told Len about it. One day when Townsend Victor was two, he tried to run out on an exercise rider, this guy named Jocko. I guess Townsend Victor actually hit another horse pretty hard. That horse had to be taken out of training and never made it to the track."

"That's terrible!" Heather sounded shocked.

"Yeah, but what happened to Townsend Victor was almost as bad. Jocko was furious when the colt got away from him, and really manhandled him. Jocko hauled on his mouth and whipped him until he bled. Townsend Victor finally threw Jocko and ran twice around the track by himself."

"That sounds almost funny," Heather said.

"It wasn't." Cindy shook her head. "Townsend Victor was always feisty, but after that he got mean. He raced a couple of times as a two-year-old and once as a three-year-old, but he only won two races. Then he got hurt in his last race when he bore out after another colt and took a misstep. He had to be retired." Cindy folded her pizza foil and stood up.

"Townsend Victor does sound like Champion," Heather said. "Champion isn't mean, but he sure is feisty."

"Well, he doesn't have the excuse for acting up that Townsend Victor did," Cindy pointed out. "Champion was born and raised at Whitebrook. Nobody's ever said a mean word to him."

"Maybe he'll straighten out when he's raced some more," Heather suggested.

"Maybe. I keep thinking that he'll do better than Townsend Victor because Champion's half Wonder—she's his dam," Cindy said. "Maybe her sweetness and willingness are buried in him somewhere."

"It should be interesting to see," Heather said.

"I'm sure of that," Cindy agreed. "Ashleigh had planned to breed Wonder again to Townsend Victor, but that won't happen now because he had to be destroyed. So Champion's unique."

Glory hopped over a log and tugged at the reins. "Okay, okay!" Cindy said, laughing. "We'll go for a gallop. I guess once a racehorse, always a racehorse, right, Glory?"

The gray stallion stepped forward eagerly, as if to say, *Now you have the right idea.*

5

On August 8, two days before Mr. Wonderful's race in the Pacific Classic, Cindy flew with Samantha to the Del Mar track.

"I can't wait to see Mr. Wonderful," Cindy said eagerly as they drove through the pretty resort town of Del Mar. Mr. Wonderful definitely had a full dose of Wonder's temperament, Cindy thought. He had always been perfect in his training. And his loving personality, so like Wonder's, had made him a favorite with everyone at Whitebrook.

Mr. Wonderful is a lot like Storm was, Cindy thought with a sigh. *I wish I could stop thinking about Storm. I can't, though. It still seems so weird the way life just goes on without him.*

For the past month Cindy had exercised Champion almost every morning. Now that Storm was gone,

Champion was the focus of her riding efforts. But after an hour or two of struggling with the erratic colt, Cindy usually needed a break from him. In the afternoons she rode Glory or one of the other horses or worked with Honor Bright. To let off steam, she complained frequently at Storm's grave about Champion. But no matter how much she tried to talk out the problem, she still seemed no closer to solving it.

Cindy worried that the colt was getting worse. Each morning she tried not to anticipate that the exercise session would go badly, but it was hard not to. Cindy hated to admit it, but in a way the trip to Del Mar was a welcome break from the frustration she was feeling about Champion.

"Mr. Wonderful is such a special horse," Samantha said, turning the rental car and pulling into the Del Mar track parking lot. "I sure hope he wins tomorrow."

"Me too. It means so much to everybody—especially Ashleigh," Cindy added. Everyone at Whitebrook knew that Ashleigh doted on the beautiful colt.

"That's true," Samantha replied. "Well, Mr. Wonderful's last workouts weren't spectacular, but the field for the Pacific Classic isn't as killer as it's been in previous years. So Mr. Wonderful probably has a good shot at winning."

Cindy felt a slight chill. *Samantha sounds like she*

thinks Mr. Wonderful will lose! I wonder why? Mr. Wonderful's performance wasn't really that bad in the Hollywood Gold Cup, she thought. He'd faded, but he still finished second.

"Is Ashleigh going to work Mr. Wonderful again before the race?" Cindy asked as they walked to the shed row.

Samantha shook her head. "Ashleigh told me last night that he's pretty much set. She took him for a gallop this morning." Samantha pointed. "There's our stabling—you'll be able to see how he is for yourself."

Cindy noticed that a crowd had gathered in front of Whitebrook's shed row. Her pulse quickened. *I hope nothing's wrong!* she thought.

"Cindy! Sammy!" The crowd parted briefly, and Ian walked toward them, a welcoming smile on his face.

Cindy realized that the crowd had gathered around Mr. Wonderful. Ashleigh was holding him while he grazed. The clear yellow California sun splashed the magnificent colt with light, turning his coat a brilliant solid gold.

Cindy gasped. "I've never seen any horse so gorgeous in my life," she said to Samantha.

"I know." Samantha nodded. "I'm sure there's never been a horse that beautiful before."

Ian reached the two girls and pulled them close for a hug. "I'm glad you're here," he said.

"Me too." Smiling, Ashleigh was leading Mr. Wonderful toward them. "I'm taking him in now," she said. "He's been out for an hour."

The spectators reluctantly parted to let the colt pass.

"May I lead him?" Cindy asked.

"Sure." Ashleigh handed her the leather lead shank. "We'll catch up with you in a minute. Ian and I need to talk to another trainer."

Mr. Wonderful whickered a happy greeting. All the attention didn't seem to have spoiled him a bit, Cindy thought. He was as gentle and friendly as ever.

Cindy saw heads turn as she led the stunning colt to the shed row. "I'd put my money on him," she heard an older man say.

"Seems a sure bet," agreed his companion, a middle-aged woman.

Mr. Wonderful walked obediently into his stall and quickly turned to face Cindy once he was inside. He seemed to be asking if there was anything else he could do.

"He's such a sweet guy," Samantha said, looking into the stall.

Cindy unexpectedly felt tears fill her eyes. Mr. Wonderful was so willing. He seemed to want nothing but to please everyone.

Cindy hugged his neck, running her fingers down

his silky golden coat. "You'll do just fine in the race," she said. "You deserve to win, boy."

The colt arched his neck and nuzzled her hair, as if to say that he would do his very best.

"Are you going riding with your friend Anne today, Cindy?" Samantha asked the next morning as she joined Cindy in the restaurant of the motel.

Cindy drained her glass of white grape juice and set it down. "Yes," she said. Cindy had met Anne Tarin at Saratoga two years ago, and the two girls had hit it off. Anne's parents were also Thoroughbred trainers. "I called Anne while you were in the shower. She and her mom will come pick me up in a few minutes. After we ride, they'll drop me back off at the track."

"Sounds good." Samantha smiled. "I guess I'll just hang out at the track and listen to the trainers talk. Sometimes you can learn a lot that way about the other horses running."

Cindy looked out the window and waved. "There's Anne and her mom!"

"Have fun," Samantha said.

"We will!" *A ride on the beach at the Pacific Ocean might be the most fun thing I've ever done!* Cindy thought as she hurried to the Tarins' car.

Dark-haired, pretty Anne Tarin was sitting in the backseat. She waved excitedly as Cindy climbed in.

50

"Hi, Cindy," said Mrs. Tarin as she started the car. "And that's probably the last word I'll get in for a while. I know you girls have a lot to talk about."

"So what's new?" Anne asked, then laughed. "I guess it'll take a while to tell me. I haven't seen you in two years."

"Not since we were running Glory in the Travers at Saratoga." Cindy smiled, remembering how Glory had set a track record in that race. But her smile faded as she remembered other big news at Whitebrook— Storm's terrible death. Cindy decided not to tell Anne unless she had heard about it and asked. Even then, Cindy didn't want to talk about it much. She doubted if she ever would. "I guess you know that Mr. Wonderful is running in the Pacific Classic on Saturday," she said.

Anne nodded. "Of course. The Pacific Classic is the talk of the town. He's going in as the favorite so far."

"Yeah, isn't it great?" Cindy smiled. "How are your horses doing?" The last time Cindy had seen Anne, her parents had just been getting some stakes-caliber horses to train.

"Really well. One of the horses my dad trained won a grade-two stakes at Arlington last month. We don't have a horse entered in the Pacific Classic, though."

Cindy reminded herself to count her blessings.

Whether Mr. Wonderful won or lost on Saturday, it was a major achievement just to run in the race. And Champion had just run in the Bashford Stakes. He had acted up, but the race was the top race for two-year-olds in the country.

"You're not going to believe my other news." Anne grinned. "I got an Arabian as a pleasure horse!"

"Wow!" Cindy didn't know much about the elegant desert horses, but she had been struck by the gorgeous looks of the ones she had seen.

Mrs. Tarin turned onto a coastal road, and Cindy could see the ocean. The waves crashed on the shore in a million sparkling points of light with a cool, refreshing sound. The smooth, glistening white beach stretched endlessly in both directions. *It's going to be really something to ride out there,* Cindy thought.

"I'll take Desert Rose, my new Arabian, on our ride," Anne said. "That's where I live." She pointed to a small cottage on a ridge just above the ocean. Behind it were a barn and a riding ring.

"You *live* there?" Cindy gasped. The cottage was practically on the water. Cindy thought it would be wonderful to fall asleep every night to the sound of the waves and wake up to the blue beauty of the ocean every morning.

Anne looked a little uncomfortable. "I know it's small—"

"It's perfect!" Cindy couldn't get over how pretty

and quaint the cottage was. "I live in a cottage, too," she added.

"For some reason I thought you lived in a mansion," Anne said.

"Nope." Cindy was already climbing out of the car. "Let's get out there! You've been promising me a ride on the beach for two years," she reminded her friend, smiling.

"I never forget my promises." Anne smiled back.

In the twelve-stall barn Anne pointed out a compact bay mare. "That's Pacific Surf, the horse I thought you could ride," she said. "She made it into the allowance ranks, and now my mom and I are reconditioning her as a pleasure horse. She's got some fire, but I figured you could handle her."

"I think so." Cindy laughed, remembering Champion's antics. *If I dare to ride Champion, I guess I'm not afraid of a nice-looking little mare!* she thought.

"What's so funny?" Anne looked at her curiously.

"I was just thinking about Wonder's Champion, a colt I'm helping to train." Cindy deftly clipped a lead line to Pacific Surf's halter and led the mare to a set of crossties. "He's a handful."

"I've heard of him," Anne said. "Anytime one of Ashleigh's Wonder's offspring runs, it's news in the Thoroughbred world. Here's Desert Rose." Anne opened a stall door and led out a magnificent white Arabian.

Cindy's eyes widened as she took in the sinuous curves of the Arabian mare and her thick, unbelievably long white mane and tail. Desert Rose was only about fifteen hands tall, but every inch of her bespoke pride and centuries of good breeding. Her well-shaped ears pricked and relaxed with nervous excitement.

"That horse looks like something out of *Arabian Nights*," Cindy said in awe.

Anne grinned and threw an English saddle over Desert Rose's back. "Wait till you see her move."

"Ready?" Cindy had already saddled Pacific Surf. She quickly mounted up. The regular English saddle felt very large compared to the tiny, light exercise saddles she used on the horses in training at Whitebrook.

Pacific Surf pranced a little on her front feet and edged sideways.

"Oh, you're not fooling me," Cindy soothed. "You're a nice girl." The mare definitely had a spark in her eye, but it was nothing like the sheer mischief in Champion's expression, she thought.

"This way to the ocean," Anne said. The horses' hooves sank deep into the sand as they rode away from the barn. Pacific Surf walked energetically, bowing her neck. She almost seemed to be watching her hoofprints. "The sand is great for conditioning horses," Anne remarked.

"I'll bet." Cindy gathered the reins. "Do you want to gallop?" she asked.

"Let's go!" In a flash Anne took off on Desert Rose, flying across the sand. Pacific Surf charged after them. The foam spray splashed into Cindy's face as Pacific Surf skimmed through the shallow water. Laughing, Cindy urged the mare to overtake Desert Rose, but the fleet Arabian was too quick. The horses' hooves dug deep into sand as they flew across the glittering beach. Looking back, Cindy saw the horses' hoofprints rapidly being erased by the incoming tide.

Pacific Surf skipped sideways to avoid a pile of driftwood. Cindy easily adjusted her balance and urged the mare on through the pounding surf.

The sharp breeze whipped back Cindy's blond hair, and her lips tasted pleasantly of salt. Anne looked around and waved, and Cindy grinned broadly back.

This is so magical! she thought. *Just like when I ride Champion. The trick is, how can I tame that magic?*

6

"LISTEN TO THOSE CHEERS!" CINDY SAID EXCITEDLY THAT Saturday. A huge crowd was cheering for Mr. Wonderful as he stepped onto the Del Mar track in the post parade for the Pacific Classic. Mr. Wonderful was an incredibly beautiful horse, but today he looked beyond beautiful. His strides were easy and graceful, and a puff of wind ruffled his thick golden mane and tail. *The day couldn't be brighter,* Cindy thought, gazing up at the azure sky. *Mr. Wonderful's chances of winning are great!*

"He looks like a champ," Beth said, smiling.

"Doesn't he?" Cindy leaned forward in her seat, studying the colt. She couldn't see a thing wrong with him.

"What's the race strategy for Mr. Wonderful?" Anne asked. Cindy had asked her friend to come to the race with her.

56

"Ashleigh will try to keep him to the front," Ian answered, leaning around Beth. Kevin sat in his lap, shaded by a cute sunbonnet.

"Is that where Mr. Wonderful usually runs?" Anne asked.

Mike frowned slightly. "Yes. But we don't want to take a chance that he'll get shuffled back in the pack, the way he did in the Gold Cup."

Cindy winced. She hoped Mike still had confidence in the colt. *I do*, she thought. *Just look at him!*

Ashleigh walked Mr. Wonderful toward the starting gate. "Ashleigh is *so* cool," Anne said.

"Isn't she?" Cindy always felt proud that she knew Ashleigh so well.

Cindy quickly looked over the field for the Pacific Classic one more time before the horses loaded in the gate. Just five other horses were running in the race, and only Mr. Wonderful had won a grade-one stakes before. My Friend Robbie, a striking reddish chestnut colt, had won the Dwyer Stakes at Belmont by a wide margin in early July. But he had just been brought in from New York last week, and he might not take to the California track, Cindy thought. Saturnalia, a tall, black colt, had won the Arkansas Derby in the spring but hadn't raced since. He might be slower than usual coming off such a long layoff.

I don't think Mr. Wonderful is going to need much help

in this race, Cindy said to herself as the colt walked confidently into the gate.

"That's Wild Ambition." Samantha pointed to a brown colt with one white stocking. "He's won only two races."

"I don't think he really belongs with this field," Mike said.

Cindy looked at the odds board. Wild Ambition, a Florida bred, was going in at odds of thirty to one.

Mike's probably right that Wild Ambition doesn't belong here, she thought. *One of those races he won was against Emeritus, the Kentucky Derby winner, but Emeritus was just coming off an injury. And that was just an allowance race. It's not like Mr. Wonderful's winning the Donn.*

Cindy looked at Samantha. "What do you think about Mr. Wonderful's chances?" she asked.

"I think they're great," Samantha said confidently. "He's the best horse with the best rider, isn't he?"

"For sure." Cindy nodded. Whatever happened, she always had confidence in Ashleigh.

"The horses are in the gate," the announcer called.

For just a moment the thousands of spectators at the huge track were almost completely still, as if they were holding their breath. Cindy gripped her program tighter, silently willing Mr. Wonderful to run his fastest.

The bell clanged into the quiet. "And they're off!"

the announcer said. "It's My Friend Robbie on the lead, with Mr. Wonderful up close second. Back three to Saturnalia; Saint Joe's and Wild Ambition running fourth and fifth."

"That's okay," Cindy said to herself as the horses swept around the first turn. "Just stay up there with them, Mr. Wonderful!"

Mr. Wonderful was running with his trademark long strides, his coat sparkling in the flooding sunlight. Cindy could almost feel the power and rhythm of the colt's strides as he gathered himself then lifted, soaring through the air.

"Is Ashleigh rating him?" Cindy asked, not taking her eyes off the field.

"I don't think so," Ian said. "Mr. Wonderful just knows what to do, and he's staying off the pace. He'll have something left in the stretch."

The six horses in the field held their positions almost perfectly as they streaked across the backstretch and plunged into the far turn. Cindy's heart beat faster. Only a quarter mile was left in the race. Now was the time for Mr. Wonderful to make his move!

As if Ashleigh heard Cindy's thoughts, she crouched farther over Mr. Wonderful's withers, asking for speed. The colt responded instantly, changing leads as he whipped into the stretch and roared up on My Friend Robbie.

"Mr. Wonderful has taken the lead!" the announcer called. "But look out! Here comes the long shot, Wild Ambition!"

Wild Ambition shot ahead like a rocket on Mr. Wonderful's outside. In barely seconds Wild Ambition had cut Mr. Wonderful's lead to a length.

Cindy could hardly believe her eyes. *Where did he come from?* she thought.

"I hope Ashleigh sees him!" Anne cried.

"She has." Cindy jumped to her feet. "She's asking Mr. Wonderful for all he's got. C'mon, boy!" she screamed. "Do it—we know you can!"

Wild Ambition was rapidly moving up at Mr. Wonderful's flank. Then the two horses were neck and neck, with only strides to the wire.

Suddenly Mr. Wonderful dropped off the pace. "No!" Cindy cried. "Not now!" But she saw that the colt couldn't make up enough ground even if he somehow fired. Wild Ambition roared under the wire. The Pacific Classic was over, with Mr. Wonderful fighting to keep second. Cindy saw unhappily that Saturnalia had almost caught him.

Cindy heard a collective groan from the crowd. Mr. Wonderful was a special favorite of many race goers, and he had let them down. *What happened?* she wondered dismally.

No one in the Whitebrook group said anything for a few seconds. Their faces were stunned and sad.

"Well, let's get down there," Ian finally said. "We've got a horse to take care of."

Silently Cindy followed her dad out of the stands. She wanted to ask him why he thought Mr. Wonderful had lost, but the discouraged expression on his face stopped her. *I'll ask Ashleigh later*, she thought. *Unless Mr. Wonderful is hurt, she'd be the one who knows best what happened.*

"I'm sorry, Cindy," Anne whispered. "He still ran a pretty good race."

"Yeah," Cindy said. She didn't agree, but she knew Anne was trying to make her feel better.

When she got to the track, Cindy went immediately to Mr. Wonderful, dodging the press, trainer, and owners who had gathered with happy expressions around Wild Ambition. "Come here, sweetheart," she called.

Mr. Wonderful looked very tired. His white-flecked neck gleamed with sweat, and his head drooped. He quickly lifted it as Cindy stepped close to him and rubbed his muzzle gently against her hands. He seemed to be saying that no matter what, he would remember his good manners and welcome her. Cindy's heart wrenched. She stroked his wet neck. "I know you tried hard," she whispered. "It's not your fault. Nobody's mad at you."

"Are you okay, Ash?" Mike asked, looking up as Ashleigh swung out of the saddle.

61

Ashleigh nodded. Cindy saw that she was still trying to catch her breath. "That was a hard ride," she said. "I think we both gave it everything we had. It just wasn't enough today."

"Let's talk about it in the shed row." Mike reached for the colt's reins.

"Come on, everybody," Beth said encouragingly.

I guess we're all standing around as if we're paralyzed, Cindy thought. *But it's just so hard to believe that Mr. Wonderful lost!*

"I'll lead him," she said. Mr. Wonderful followed obediently, occasionally touching Cindy's hand with his nose. Ashleigh walked on the other side of the colt with her hand on his shoulder.

"I'm afraid that's it for him as a racehorse," she said quietly. "We'll retire him to stud." She dropped back to talk to Mike.

Cindy swallowed hard. She felt terrible for Ashleigh. "At least he isn't hurt," Cindy said to Anne. "And he had a great career for a while."

"You could always run him in minor stakes races or allowance races," Anne suggested.

Cindy shook her head. "I don't think Ashleigh will want to do that. I mean, it would be such a letdown. I guess we'll just take him home. Then he'll be bred next winter."

"When do you go back to Whitebrook?" Anne asked.

Cindy tried to think. She was so disappointed about Mr. Wonderful, she could hardly focus on anything else. "Tomorrow," she said finally. "Dad and Mike will stay out here, but Ashleigh's coming home with the rest of us. She doesn't want to be away from her daughter, Christina, for too long."

"I've got to find my parents now," Anne said. "But stop off at our place and say good-bye tomorrow. Maybe we can go for another quick ride."

Cindy smiled a little. "I'll see if we have time," she said. Anne was being so nice. But Cindy wondered if even a ride on the beach would be any fun now.

In the shed row Cindy held Mr. Wonderful while Mike, Ashleigh, and Ian carefully examined him, paying particular attention to his legs.

"There's no damage that I can see," Mike said at last. "We'll get him vetted again, but he seems okay for now."

"I'll cool him out," Cindy offered.

"Thanks, Cindy," Ashleigh said. "I've got to straighten out some paperwork with the racing secretary. I'll be back as soon as I can."

Ashleigh looked very depressed, Cindy thought. She couldn't blame her. In just a day Mr. Wonderful, the star of Whitebrook, had ended his racing career. Some of Whitebrook's two-year-olds who were coming along seemed promising, like Limitless Time, but none of them had proved themselves yet.

Except Champion, Cindy thought. *He's Wonder's son and Mr. Wonderful's half-brother. Now it's up to him to carry on Wonder's line of racing champions.*

Cindy carefully cooled out Mr. Wonderful, then checked with her dad to see if the colt could go back in his stall.

"He looks fine," Ian said. "Thanks, honey."

"I'll stay in the stall with him until Ashleigh gets back." Cindy let Mr. Wonderful walk into the stall ahead of her.

Ian nodded. "Good. I think he needs a little consolation." Ian smiled ruefully. "Maybe we all do."

Cindy topped off Mr. Wonderful's water bucket, then shook out several sheaves of straw on the floor of the stall so that the colt would be comfortable. The barn seemed strangely quiet. Len hadn't come along to Del Mar, and for once none of the press were crowding in the aisle, asking for interviews. They were all at Wild Ambition's stall, Cindy realized.

"Now what should I do?" she said aloud. Working on the stall had taken her mind off the race for a few minutes, but now she was alone with her thoughts. Cindy slumped against the wall and slid to the ground. Always the gentleman, Mr. Wonderful stepped over to her and gently nuzzled her hair, as if he were trying to comfort her.

Cindy lifted a hand and ran it through his golden

mane. "What happened, boy?" she asked softly. "I'm not blaming you. I just want to know."

Mr. Wonderful's big brown eyes were bright as he gazed at her. Cindy affectionately rubbed his star. "Whatever it was, I know you tried your best," she said.

The best horse, with the best rider. Samantha's words came back to Cindy. "Why wasn't that enough for you to win?" she asked Mr. Wonderful. "It should have been." That was true for Champion, too, she realized. He was an extremely talented colt, and Ashleigh was also his jockey.

"You went from winning grade-one races to not being able to keep up with the leaders." Cindy stood and walked around the colt. With his perfect conformation and burnished coat, Mr. Wonderful looked the same as always. But she knew that Thoroughbreds were highly sensitive, both mentally and physically. If Mr. Wonderful was off even a little, it would have ruined his chances in the race.

Something has happened to you and also to Champion, Cindy thought. *If I can't figure out what's wrong with Champion, his racing career may be over soon, too.*

7

"OKAY, CHAMPION, SHOW ME WHAT YOU CAN DO," CINDY said two days later as she tightened the girth on the colt's saddle. She had returned to Whitebrook from Del Mar on Sunday night, the day after the Pacific Classic. After Mr. Wonderful's loss in the race, Cindy was more determined than ever to turn Champion's training around.

Champion pawed a hoof briefly on the cement stable aisle, then twisted his head as far around as he could in the crossties to look at her. *At least he seems very interested in what I'm saying,* Cindy thought. *Now the question is whether he'll do what I say.*

"He is one fine-looking horse," Len said, coming down the aisle with a wheelbarrow.

"Isn't he?" Cindy stepped back to admire her grooming work. Champion's coat was the color of thick chocolate pudding, and his star and blaze were bright satiny white on his dark brown face. "You look like a champion," she told him with a smile.

Champion's ears pricked. He quivered, then stamped his hoof.

"Let's go release some of that energy," Cindy said, unclipping the crossties and gathering the colt's reins. "But let's do it right, Champion. No tricks."

The colt huffed out a breath, as if he would never dream of such a thing. Cindy smiled as she led him out of the barn into the cool morning.

It had rained the night before, and the air was clean and fresh. The newly risen sun touched the tops of the low, rolling hills with clear yellow.

"What a day!" Cindy said, taking a deep breath. Ahead of them she could see Mike leaning on the rail as he watched the horses in training on the track. Ashleigh and Samantha were galloping Freedom's Ring and Limitless Time through the golden light. The young colts moved together almost as one. Their action was so graceful, only the quick sound of their snorted breaths gave any clue to their speed.

Champion tugged firmly on the reins as he and Cindy reached the gap. The colt stopped and looked straight ahead, every muscle tense.

"You really are gorgeous," Cindy said softly. The powerful colt was silhouetted against the big yellow sun. As he shifted his weight his coat burst into a million glittering points of shimmering brown. Bracing his long, slender legs, Champion stood perfectly square, gazing at the track. His eyes were bright, as if he knew exactly what was ahead of him.

I wonder what is ahead of him? she thought. *He has that eye-catching quality, that presence, that great horses are said to have. It's getting stronger as he grows up.* "Oh, Champion," she whispered. "I know you can be one of the greatest stars Whitebrook has ever had. We've just got to get out there and prove it, boy."

Champion whinnied sharply. A few seconds later Ashleigh and Samantha rode Freedom's Ring and Limitless Time over to the gap.

"Look at you, Champion," Samantha said. "What a pretty boy."

"He does look fantastic this morning." Cindy stretched forward in the stirrups to rub the colt's neck.

"He's as pretty as Mr. Wonderful," Ashleigh said. "Well, almost," she said with a rueful laugh. "I have to admit I'm partial."

"Champion's . . . kind of wilder than Mr. Wonderful, though, isn't he?" Cindy said slowly. Sometimes she thought Champion had more spirit than Mr. Wonderful. But she didn't want to hurt Ashleigh's feelings by saying so, especially when Mr. Wonderful had faded in his last race. *Besides, I'm not sure if all that spirit is a good thing if Champion doesn't use it to run faster!* she thought.

Ashleigh hopped off Freedom's Ring and caught the colt's reins. "Handsome is as handsome does," she said, seeming to read Cindy's mind. "Okay, take Champion around, Cindy."

"How come Champion isn't going out with Limitless and Freedom?" Cindy asked.

"I want to see how he'll do without any distractions," Ashleigh said.

"Let's keep the workout simple," Mike added, walking over to the group. "Just a slow gallop twice around, Cindy. Keep Champion in hand."

"I'll take these two guys to the barn," Samantha said, reaching for Freedom's reins.

"Thanks." Ashleigh leaned against the rail with Mike. Mike put his arm around Ashleigh's shoulders. *I think Ashleigh still feels really bad about Mr. Wonderful,* Cindy thought with a pang. Dr. Smith had thoroughly examined the colt but still hadn't found anything wrong with him. Cindy knew it was very difficult for Ashleigh to accept that Mr. Wonderful might have just quit on her.

Cindy shook her head as she cued Champion to walk counterclockwise around the track. She still felt terrible about Mr. Wonderful, too, but she had a horse to exercise. "Let's put in a good workout today, Champion," she said. "We want to show Ashleigh what she wants to see."

"Cindy, wait a minute!" Vic Teleski, one of

Whitebrook's full-time grooms, was just leaving the track on Border South, a three-year-old gray filly who had won an allowance race last week at Ellis Park. Vic trotted Border South after them. "I took Champion out while you were at Del Mar," he said.

"How did he do?" Cindy looked at Vic in surprise. Champion didn't care for a lot of people, but he really disliked Vic. No one knew why. Cindy knew that the feeling was mutual. *Mike must have twisted Vic's arm to get him to exercise Champion*, she thought.

Vic grimaced. "Do you really want to know what he did?"

Cindy looked down at the colt. Champion was chomping on the bit and watching Border South and Vic. He seemed to be listening, too. "Yes," she said. "That might help me figure out what he's plotting today." Cindy used to think it was silly to talk about a horse plotting, but she had long since decided that Champion was so smart, he plotted all the time.

"He was all right for about a minute on Friday," Vic said.

Cindy nodded. That sounded like Champion. "Then what?" she asked.

"He gave me the works," Vic said. "Bucking, bearing in and out, running off. Then he settled down again. I thought, Phew, he's gotten all that extra energy out of his system."

Cindy was sure there was more to the story. As far

as she knew, Champion had an inexhaustible supply of energy. "Then what happened?" she asked.

"He took off bucking again." Vic sighed. "I tried to sit out the bucks, but he threw me good after about a quarter mile. Then he took off by himself. At least he didn't hit anything or run into the rail."

"No, he wouldn't do that," Cindy said. Last spring when Cindy had been riding Champion, he had crashed into the inside rail and fallen, throwing her. The intelligent colt had taken Cindy for wild rides since, but he had never run into the rail again.

"Well, that's it," Vic said, reining in Border South and turning her. "Good luck."

Cindy could feel her heart sinking as Vic rode off. Champion's behavior for Vic sounded even more diabolical than usual. The colt had pulled two major tricks instead of just one. Champion might not be improving his running skills, but his skill for causing trouble seemed to be getting sharper all the time. "Okay, Champion," she said. "I wonder what's in store for me now?"

Maybe it's good that he's so feisty, she thought. *The sweet-tempered horses like Mr. Wonderful and Storm seem to end up losing or dead.* Cindy sighed.

The dark chestnut colt floated at the trot, his neck arched and his ears flicked back, awaiting her commands. He was being a model horse, but Cindy wasn't deceived. Despite the early morning cool,

71

Champion's neck was already sweated up. He seemed to be looking all over the track instead of straight ahead.

"Here we go, boy," Cindy said determinedly after they had lapped the track at a trot. "We're going to do a slow gallop—and I do mean *slow*."

In an instant Champion bounded into a gallop. Despite her misgivings, Cindy couldn't help admiring the ease of his long, measured strides. His motion was so smooth, it was almost like that of a gaited horse. Cindy could hardly tell that they were at a gallop except that the harrowed dirt of the track rushed by beneath them. Champion was sweating freely and bowing his neck, indicating his displeasure at being held back. But so far he was doing everything she asked.

"Let's pick it up just a little, Champion," Cindy said. She hoped that the colt would glide into the faster pace, treating her to a brilliant change of action.

She let out Champion's reins a notch. The colt gave a sharp snort, then broke into a jagged gallop, running out toward the center of the track.

Oh, no! Immediately Cindy pulled Champion's head to the inside, but his legs and body were still pointed to the outside. He skittered across the track toward the outside rail.

Champion's not going to do any miracle changes of gear, Cindy realized with alarm. *I'll be lucky to get us through this work in one piece!* "Not again," she cried. "Champion, just stop it!"

The tension in her voice only seemed to make the colt worse. His tail flicking with agitation, Champion yanked at the reins, hauling them across the track.

The outside rail loomed. Cindy could almost touch it with her boot. *Are we going into it?* she thought frantically. *Champion's never run into the outside rail—maybe he wants to try it!*

At the last possible second the colt veered away, plunging toward the middle of the track. Cindy bit back a cry as Champion's abrupt motion almost threw her and she lost a stirrup.

"I won't fall!" she whispered. "We're in this together, Champion, no matter what you do!" But she knew that one more lurch in the colt's strides would unseat her. She was missing a stirrup, and she couldn't regain her balance at the irregular gallop. Only her one hand, wrapped tightly in Champion's mane, was holding her on.

Champion's ears flicked back. He seemed to have heard her quiet voice. His gallop was still jagged, and the whites of his eyes showed as he looked around the track, but he was going in a straight line. He was under control—if just barely.

"Okay!" Cindy said breathlessly. "That's better, Champion." Slowly she shifted her weight over the colt's back until she was almost centered. She didn't dare bend to try to regain her stirrup.

"Bring him over!" Ashleigh called.

Cindy pulled Champion up at the gap. Her heart was thundering, not with fear for herself but for the colt. *We were so close to that rail*, she thought, *so close to disaster.* "I'm sorry," she said to Ashleigh and Mike. Her voice quivered with strain, and she almost fell as she dismounted.

"It's not your fault—that was good riding." Ashleigh blew out a deep sigh.

"Maybe you should take him around," Cindy said. After all, Ashleigh had a lot more experience riding than she did.

"Maybe. But he does the same thing for me." Ashleigh tugged her hair. "Our current approach to his training isn't working. I'll keep thinking what else we can try with him, but you think, too, Cindy. You know him best."

Cindy looked at Champion. "Maybe you should *stop* thinking," she said to the colt. "That's what gets us into all this trouble."

Champion bumped her carelessly with his nose, as if to say that he didn't have a problem with the morning's performance.

"Cool him out well," Ashleigh said. "He's really hot."

"Okay." Cindy led the colt toward the shed row. Champion danced at the end of the reins, still full of high spirits. He seemed to be enjoying the fact that he'd just gotten his way again, Cindy thought with annoyance. "You think you're smarter than I am, Champion," she said. "But you're not going to outwit me forever. I can promise you that."

"I'm ready to do something else," Cindy said to Heather later that morning as she slipped down from the paddock fence. Cindy had been sitting on the fence for almost two hours, watching Champion cavort across the paddock and trying to come up with new training ideas for him. She still didn't have a clue what she should try now.

This is so discouraging, she thought as Champion circled the paddock at a trot, seeming to stake out his territory.

Cindy had taken one break from her vigil to call Heather, inviting her to come over and play with the foals and go for a ride. Cindy had barely managed to stop herself from spending the morning out in Storm's field, relaxing in her memories. The situation with Champion was serious, she had reminded herself. She really had to devote her full attention to it.

Cindy mopped her blond hair off her forehead. The day was nice, clear and not humid, but the July sun was very hot.

"Champion acted up again?" Heather said sympathetically as they walked to the mares' and foals' paddock.

"He was a bear," Cindy said. She really couldn't think how to describe Champion's behavior, but he certainly hadn't acted like a normal horse. She shook her head. "I don't know *what* went wrong. I was really psyched for a great workout with him. Or I guess I was, until Vic told me everything Champion did wrong for him."

"This whole thing sounds weird," Heather said. "The way he's been acting doesn't have any pattern."

"Well, I realized this morning that I shouldn't yell at him," Cindy said. "He really hates it. I didn't mean to yell, but we were about to hit the rail."

"Then you didn't have any choice," Heather said.

"I guess not, but it was still a mistake." Cindy frowned. *Another mistake,* she thought. *I make too many with him.*

Honor Bright already stood at the paddock gate, her small head cocked alertly. Lined up on either side of her were the two black fillies, Fleet Street and Lucky Chance. Honor's bright bay coat seemed even more brilliant as she stood next to the two coal-colored fillies.

Cindy's heart melted at the sweet, hopeful expressions on the foals' faces. The fillies wore tiny halters on their exquisite little heads. "Fleet Street and Lucky Chance are the honor guard," Cindy said with a smile.

"Those three do seem to be best friends," Heather agreed.

"Let's work with these guys." Cindy opened the gate just wide enough to get through. "I hope whatever happened with Champion doesn't happen to them."

"Do you think it will?" Heather looked surprised.

"I don't know. That's what's frustrating about Champion." Cindy shook her head. "I was starting to think I knew a little about training Thoroughbreds. But now I feel like I'm messing him up."

"Nobody else thinks that or you wouldn't be riding him," Heather pointed out.

"I guess. But I still feel like I'm letting him down." Cindy pulled a carrot out of her pocket and broke it into three pieces.

Honor pushed eagerly forward, bobbing her head. "You can be first," Cindy said with a laugh, handing Heather a piece of carrot for Fleet Street. Honor's soft muzzle tickled Cindy's hand as the foal delicately lipped up the carrot.

The other eight foals in the band moseyed over, eyeing the treat. "Yes, I brought enough for everybody," Cindy said. She didn't want to play favorites.

"This is fun!" Heather stood at the center of a circle of foals, handing out carrots.

"Hey, don't push." Cindy laughed as Jazz Rhythm, one of the two colts, eagerly nudged her hand, asking for his share.

Honor pinned back her small ears and took a menacing step toward the bigger foal.

"Look, Honor's sticking up for you!" Heather said.

"Easy, girl." Cindy patted the filly's neck. "You don't need to fight for me—I can take care of myself."

Honor ears stayed pinned, almost touching her small head. Jazz Rhythm backed away, but not before snatching his carrot from Cindy's hand. Honor's ears came up a fraction.

"Do you spend a lot of time with her?" Heather asked as Cindy clipped a lead line to the filly's halter.

"Pretty much. I divide my time between Champion, Honor, and chores," Cindy replied. *And Storm*, she added to herself. Cindy supposed Ashleigh and Samantha had guessed how much time she still spent at Storm's grave, but she didn't want to tell anyone else, not even Heather. Cindy knew she should be over his death by now.

"That sounds like enough time for her," Heather said.

"Do you want to lead Fleet Street?" Cindy asked. "She's pretty gentle."

"Sure!" Heather said eagerly. She hurried to the gate for another lead line, then attached it to Fleet Street's halter. The filly stood calmly. Cindy knew that Ashleigh spent a lot of time with Fleet Street. The filly was used to attention.

"I love the way we can be with the horses all day

78

in the summer," Cindy said as she led Honor Bright around the fence line. The filly trotted lightly after her. Young as Honor was, her trot was almost perfectly coordinated. "After this, let's go see Glory and Pride," she added. "Then we can saddle up and go out on the trails."

"Okay." Heather nodded. "We'd better ride a lot while we have time. We start school in just a couple of weeks. Ninth grade—wow! We'll be in high school. That's kind of scary."

"It'll be fun to be in a new school, though, with older kids," Cindy said. "And I can't wait to see Max again and hear about his summer."

"Look around you," Heather said with a grin.

Cindy glanced over her shoulder and saw that the entire troop of foals was following them. Jostling a bit, but mostly in orderly pairs of two, the foals all stepped along behind Honor and Fleet Street as if they were in a parade. "You silly little guys," Cindy said fondly.

In the distance a dog barked. Honor braced her long legs comically and stared fearfully in the direction of the danger.

"It's okay, baby." Cindy ran her hand reassuringly along Honor's short back. She let the filly stand as long as she needed to.

With a little snort Honor walked on. Then she broke into a trot again and caught up to Cindy, walking next to her instead of behind. "So we're partners?" Cindy asked. She stopped to hug the foal.

Honor touched Cindy's ear with her unbelievably soft muzzle and huffed out a little sigh. She seemed to be saying, *Forever, pal.*

"Cindy, where are you going?" Beth asked that night, looking up from the book she was reading in the McLeans' living room. "It's so late."

Cindy stopped and looked at her watch. It was after ten o'clock. "Just out to the barn. I want to talk to Champion for a minute."

Beth smiled. "Okay, sweetheart. But don't stay long if you plan to get up early tomorrow to work with the horses."

"I won't." Cindy closed the door behind her and walked down the path to the training barn. She hadn't wanted to go to bed that night without seeing the colt. She felt that they hadn't parted on a good note at all that day.

The warm late summer air, thick with the smell of raspberries and dew-drenched flowers, wrapped around her like a blanket. *Summer's almost over,* Cindy thought. *In just three weeks Champion races again.*

In the quiet, dimly lit barn most of the horses were asleep, standing up. She could hear the soft rustle of straw as a few restless horses shifted position.

Champion was in the shadows at the back of his stall. "Hey, boy," she said softly. "Were you asleep?"

The colt's eyes were bright in the near darkness. Cindy could tell he hadn't been asleep. Like Glory, he didn't seem to need much sleep.

Cindy let herself into the stall and turned to look at Champion. In the yellow glow from the barn night-lights the colt's coat gleamed a rich, velvety brown. "What's the problem, boy?" she murmured. "Why do you act the way you do?"

Champion eyed her warily, as if he didn't appreciate the criticism.

"Come here," Cindy said, stretching her hand out to him. "I still like you, even if you almost threw me again today."

Champion took a step toward her, then spooked at a *thump* on the top of the narrow half door. The McLeans' big gray cat fought for balance. Regaining it, he paced on top of the door.

"That's just Imp," Cindy reassured the colt. "I guess he heard me in here, because at night he usually stays in the stallion barn with Glory."

Champion stepped to the front of the stall and sniffed the cat dubiously. "You don't have a cat friend, do you?" Cindy asked the colt. "I'm really your best friend. And if you don't quit this nonsense at the track, I may be your *only* friend."

Champion rubbed his head on her shirt, his ears

81

relaxed. *I hardly ever see him so calm,* Cindy thought. Imp sat down on the door and stared at them with unblinking green eyes, as if he were watching the peace process. "So why won't you do what I want, Champion?" Cindy asked. "I know you're basically a sweet boy."

She reached to pat Imp. The cat arched his back and purred throatily.

Cindy glanced out at the silent aisle. The dark squares above each stall half door hid the horses inside. *What will come out of the shadows?* she wondered. *Where will Champion be in a year?* Would he be Whitebrook's new star at the track or just a midlevel racehorse, one nobody talked about much? Or would he be a failure, his place in the sun taken by one of the other young horses in training?

Imp jumped off the stall door and headed back to Glory. Cindy snapped back to the present as Champion dropped his sleek head into her arms for a hug.

He likes me and he trusts me, she said to herself. *I shouldn't have a problem with him. But I do.*

8

On September 1, the day of the Juvenile Stakes at Ellis Park, Cindy, Ashleigh, and Samantha watched while Ian and Len took Champion around the walking ring. *This time we've got the walking ring all to ourselves,* Cindy thought with a frown.

The men were each holding the colt with a lead rope, one on each side. Ian had gotten permission from the track stewards to take Champion out of the saddling paddock by himself, before the other horses. Cindy knew, though, that the track officials' patience with Champion would wear out soon. Then no special exceptions would be made for him.

Champion grabbed Len's lead rope in his mouth and chewed on it, rolling a wild dark eye at the crowd. The day was overcast and cool, but the excited colt's neck and flanks were already dark with sweat. No rain had fallen yet, although the thick scent of summer rain was in the air. The track was listed as fast. Cindy wondered how Champion would do on an off track. Someday he would have to run on one. *He really is just beginning as a racehorse*, she thought. *There's a lot we don't know about him yet.*

"Champion's acting the same way he did before the Bashford," Samantha said. "He's all wound up."

Ashleigh nodded, not taking her eyes off the colt. She was wearing Whitebrook's blue-and-white colors and seemed deep in thought.

"Champion doesn't act that way at home," Cindy said. With increasing frustration she watched the colt nervously pace after her dad and Len. Cindy walked Champion around Whitebrook almost every day. Usually he got a little fidgety, but nothing like this. *What's wrong with him?* she asked herself.

Champion stopped to survey his surroundings, his neck arched alertly, his bright eyes scanning the crowd. Tossing his heavy dark mane, he sidestepped, swinging his back hooves dangerously near the onlookers.

"Is he reacting to the crowd?" Samantha asked.

"Maybe." Cindy had noticed that the walking ring was filled with people, even more so than it had been at the Bashford. "I wonder if everyone came here because they thought Champion would act up?"

"If they did, they're getting a great show," Samantha said grimly.

Cindy bit back a cry as Champion half reared, twisting toward the onlookers. Ian quickly brought the colt down and led him over to Ashleigh.

"He's never reared in the walking ring." Ashleigh shook her head. "He sure is inventive."

Give Ashleigh a break, Champion! Cindy thought, looking sympathetically at his jockey. Mr. Wonderful had been losing weight since the Pacific Classic, and everyone at Whitebrook was concerned about him. But Ashleigh was worried almost to death.

"Troubles never come singly," Beth had said. Looking at Champion now, Cindy had to agree.

Cindy took a deep breath and tried to calm herself while Ashleigh checked the saddle girth, then quickly hopped into the saddle with a hand from Ian. *I want to say something to Champion before he goes out on the track*, Cindy thought. *But I can't get angry or excited with him, even if he isn't behaving very well. He'll just pick up on it and act worse.*

Cindy knew she didn't have much time. The other horses in the field were circling the walking ring, and Ashleigh had to get Champion out to the track before the rest of the field joined them. "Champion, please settle down," she said.

The colt butted her rudely with his nose, then jumped in place. Ashleigh went with him, easily keeping her balance. "That's enough," Ian said firmly, tightening his grip on the reins. Champion chewed on the bit, but he stood in one place, lightly pawing with one hoof.

"Well, I think I know what to expect out there." Ashleigh adjusted her feet in the stirrups.

"Be careful," Mike said quietly. Cindy knew that he worried about Ashleigh when she rode in races. Even under the best circumstances horse racing was dangerous—thousand-pound horses fought for position at very high speeds.

And these aren't the best circumstances, Cindy thought. Ashleigh smiled bravely at Mike, then tried to turn Champion toward the track. The colt was looking at Cindy, his dark eyes expectant, almost as if he had something to say. Cindy tried desperately to think if there was anything she could do to make a difference in the outcome of the race. With every minute that passed, she was getting more and more worried about it.

"Just run, Champion," she said finally. "That's all you have to do. You know what we want."

"See you," Ashleigh said, and decisively turned the colt toward the track. With her back straight, she and the colt disappeared into the tunnel.

"Let's get up to the stands." Cindy was already hurrying toward the grandstand.

"Hi, everybody," Beth greeted them as they took seats beside her. "Champion just walked out on the track. He seems to be doing better."

"I hope so," Cindy said. "But I'm not sure he's through acting up."

"Ashleigh can handle him." Samantha sounded confident.

Cindy saw that Ashleigh was keeping Champion clear of the other horses in the post parade. The colt seemed to be responding to her well.

"There's a lot of speed in this race," Ian remarked. "Cajun King and Golden Patriot have both won at seven furlongs."

"Ashleigh will have to give Champion time to close," Mike said. "The race is relatively short, and Champion isn't a speed horse."

Storm was, Cindy thought unhappily. *He may have been the fastest speed horse ever!* She remembered how proud and confident she had been as the gray colt soared through sprints last spring, one of the fastest horses in the world. *I wish he were still alive.*

Cindy shook her head, swallowing back her feeling of disappointment. Champion was Wonder's son, and the brightest hope of Whitebrook now. She had to stop comparing him to Storm.

"Champion's in the five position in a nine-horse field," Samantha said, turning to Ian. "Is Ashleigh going to try to take him straight to the rail?"

"Not if the traffic's too heavy," Ian said. "We'll have to see how the field breaks from the gate. If

87

Champion gets away sharply, maybe he can get right to the inside."

"The horses are in the gate," the announcer called. Cindy strained to see Champion. The horses were loading on the far side of the track, and she could barely see his head, but he seemed to standing on all four feet, almost calmly. "And they're off!"

Champion lunged out of the gate. "That's right, boy!" Cindy cried. Sliding to the edge of her seat, she quickly focused her binoculars. "Get a jump on those other horses!" The colt was up close behind the front-runners, Cajun King and Golden Patriot, who had broken from the two and three positions.

Suddenly Champion veered sharply and ran straight across the track toward the inside rail. "Oh, my God!" Cindy bit back a scream.

"Ashleigh can't stop him in time," Samantha gasped.

But in an instant Ashleigh pulled the colt's head around hard, forcing him to straighten out. Champion almost lost his balance but gathered his legs under him. Finally the dark chestnut colt bounded after the rest of the field.

"Why couldn't he run like that in the first place?" Cindy was out of breath, as if she were running the race, too.

"Champion's last by six lengths!" Beth sounded dismayed.

"No wonder." Cindy stood on tiptoes, trying to see the horses coming into the far turn. "I thought we got him over running into rails!"

"Champion's still relatively inexperienced," Mike reminded her. "He may have overreacted to Ashleigh's direction to go to the rail."

Cindy nodded, looking through her binoculars. Now she could hear the sound of nine Thoroughbreds running flat out, the drumming of their hoofbeats like the onrush of a rainstorm. No matter how many races she had been to, Cindy still loved the sound. "Here comes Champion!" she cried. The colt had switched leads coming into the stretch. In a couple of strides he had caught the trailers and was bearing down on Cajun King and Golden Patriot.

"Wonder's Champion has rallied from last," the announcer called. "He's making his move on the inside."

"Now we'll see if Cajun King and Golden Patriot have enough left to hang on to the wire," Ian said.

"*Don't* go at the rail again, Champion," Cindy said, clenching her teeth. But she could see that Champion was moving in a perfectly straight line now, surging after the horses ahead of him. "That's it," she whispered. "Go, boy!"

"He's almost on top of them!" Mike said. "I'll bet Ashleigh's having trouble."

"Wonder's Champion lacks room," the announcer called. "But he's going through on the inside!"

The colt was determined to force his way through. He was up on the heels of Cajun King and Golden Patriot coming into the stretch. Golden Patriot drifted out, tiring.

"Now's your chance—just one more horse to beat, Champion!" Cindy was sure Ashleigh would take Champion around Cajun King on the outside.

Suddenly Cajun King bore out, and Champion roared through the narrow opening at the rail. "Come on, Champion!" Cindy screamed. The colt's strides were beautifully level and even as he glided across the track. *Nothing can stop him now if he'll just keep running like that!* Cindy thought.

"Did Champion bump Cajun King or did he just veer off to avoid Champion?" Samantha asked anxiously.

"I don't know." Ian shook his head. "Either is possible. That was an aggressive move."

"Champion's going to win it!" Cindy thought she might cry with happiness. Champion was streaking for the wire, lengths ahead of Cajun King and Golden Patriot. Time had run out for his rivals to catch him— or for Champion to try another trick.

"Wonder's Champion takes the second race in the Kentucky Thoroughbred Development Fund Bonus Series," the announcer called. "He's going for three now, ladies and gentlemen."

"Wow, what a run!" Cindy couldn't stop smiling.

"It sure was," Mike said. "Let's go talk to Ashleigh."

Ashleigh had already ridden Champion back to the gap by the time the Whitebrook group reached the track. "Whew," she said, slipping out of the saddle. "That was a rough trip."

Cindy tried to look Champion over as Ian firmly gripped the colt's reins, but Champion wasn't making it easy. Still excited from the race, he danced his hindquarters in a semicircle and flung up his head.

"What happened out there?" Ian asked Ashleigh.

"Champion didn't bump Cajun King," Ashleigh said. "I may be in trouble for reckless riding, though." Ashleigh pointed to the board. The Inquiry sign was flashing.

"Danny Rodriguez, Cajun King's jockey, will have protested Champion's action in the stretch," Mike said. "The protest may stand, too."

"Oh, no," Cindy gasped. After such an effort, Champion might be stripped of his victory! But she had to admit that it might be fair.

"No surprise," Mike said with a sigh. "We'll just have to see what the stewards decide."

Ashleigh weighed in with Champion's saddle. The crowd was quiet as they waited for the stewards' decision.

After a few minutes a cheer went up from the crowd. "The stewards are letting Champion's first place stand!" Ashleigh sounded surprised.

Cindy rubbed Champion's neck. "You did well after all," she told him fondly. "I hope that's what you wanted, too."

Champion pulled firmly on the reins, as if he couldn't wait to get in the victory photograph.

"I was very lucky the stewards didn't suspend me today," Ashleigh said as she and Cindy put Champion back in his stall after the race. They had walked him around the shed row until he was completely cooled out. "The stewards decided that when Champion pushed by Cajun King in the stretch, it didn't affect the outcome of the race."

"Champion did win by a lot," Cindy said, stepping inside the stall and stroking Champion's blaze. The colt nudged her quickly and snorted, as if to say, *Don't forget it.*

"We've still got a problem with him." Ashleigh frowned and leaned over the stall door. "Cindy, I wasn't suspended this time for reckless riding, maybe because the stewards know I don't ride that way on purpose. But Champion's performance out there was alarming, to say the least. He's got a lot of bad habits on the track now."

"What do you think we should do?" Cindy realized what a brilliant ride Ashleigh had put in. Cindy was sure that only Ashleigh's skill had won the victory for Champion and averted disaster on the track.

"That's a tough one," Ashleigh said thoughtfully. "We've got three weeks to turn him around before the Kentucky Cup Juvenile Stakes at Turfway Park. Let's try exercising him hard between now and then. And I want him to run with other horses much more than he has been. Champion never seems to need competition to run his best, and other horses don't intimidate him. I don't think I paid enough attention to the fact that he likes to intimidate the competition, the way he did today."

"He does rush at other horses." Cindy stepped back to look at the colt. "You don't really care much for them, do you, Champion?" she asked. "You don't have a horse buddy."

"I'm not sure he cares much for any living creature but you," Ashleigh said with a smile. "He's really your horse."

"And yours too," Cindy said loyally. Champion looked from Cindy to Ashleigh with soft dark eyes, as if he agreed.

"I hope his trust in us helps him in the Kentucky Cup Juvenile Stakes," Ashleigh said. "At a mile and a sixteenth, with two turns, it's a much longer race than the Juvenile Stakes here. Champion will have to put his mind and heart into running to win it. He can't goof off."

Cindy remembered that a few years ago she and Ashleigh had a similar problem with Glory not always putting out his best effort on the track. But Glory had bad memories of his earlier training by abusive people.

Champion has great memories of the track—he remembers that he gets his way out there, Cindy thought. *I see what Ashleigh means about bad habits.*

Champion pricked his ears and stepped very close to Cindy. From the alert expression on his face, Cindy would have sworn he could understand what she was thinking.

I'll do whatever it takes to get you ready for the Kentucky Cup Juvenile Stakes, Cindy vowed. "Okay, Champion," she said firmly. "Here we go again. You're going to have a perfect trip the next time you run."

9

"MAX, WAIT UP!" CINDY HURRIED DOWN THE HALLWAY AT Henry Clay High School. It was the first day of school after Labor Day, and she had just caught her first glimpse of Max since the Fourth of July. Cindy couldn't wait to talk to him.

Max turned quickly at the sound of her voice. "Cindy!" he called, smiling broadly.

"You're back!" Cindy leaned against a row of lockers to catch her breath. She was almost late for her first class already because she'd taken a wrong turn in the big new high school. It was good to see Max's familiar face. "Did you have fun in Washington with your dad?" she asked.

"Yeah. We tried to fish." Max laughed. "You need a lot of patience to be a fisherman, so I didn't catch much. But my dad and I went on a lot of cool hikes in the mountains, and we went canoeing. Staying out there wasn't as bad as I thought. What's new at Whitebrook?"

"So much, I almost don't know where to begin." Cindy quickly recounted Champion's narrow victory in the Juvenile Stakes the past Saturday. "I was happy with him even though he made trouble on the backside and on the track," she said. "Ashleigh should get most of the credit. But maybe Champion's turned over a new leaf. This morning I gave him a long exercise session and he went perfectly."

"He really is moody," Max said.

"I know," Cindy agreed. "I just need to figure out how to get him in a good mood. It's sort of a puzzle."

Max was listening intently. "Maybe we can solve it," he said.

"I bet we can." Cindy nodded. *I'm so glad Max is back*, she thought happily. *I'm lucky to have such a good friend to talk to about Champion.*

The bell rang. "What's your first class?" Max asked.

"Geometry." Cindy made a face. "I don't think I'm awake enough to do math first thing every morning. Where are you going?"

"History, if I can find my classroom," Max said.

"Catch you later." Cindy turned to go the way she thought her geometry class was.

"Hey, Cindy—wait a sec. I wanted to ask you something."

Cindy stopped and looked at Max in surprise. He was blushing under his tan. *Want to ask me what?* she thought.

"Would you go to the first school dance with me?" Max cleared his throat and looked even more uncomfortable. "It's not for three weeks, but I thought I'd ask now just to make sure you could come. I mean, if you want."

Cindy stared at Max, her mouth dropping open. Max was asking her on a date! She realized he was still waiting for her reply. "Well . . . sure, I'd like to go," she said slowly. At Henry Clay Middle School Cindy and Heather had worked on the decorations committee for a couple of the dances, but they'd always been too shy to dance. *I don't even know how!* Cindy remembered. *I'm going to look like an idiot! Why is Max asking me to a dance?*

Max looked relieved. "Great," he said. "So that's settled. See you later."

"See you," Cindy said numbly. She headed off to geometry again, but she was more disoriented than ever. Suddenly she stopped dead, remembering Max's warm smile. "I know what was wrong with him on the Fourth of July," she said aloud to the almost empty hall. A few kids looked at her peculiarly. Cindy swallowed and looked away. *He wasn't upset about spending the summer with his father*, she thought. *Max likes me as a girlfriend!*

*   *   *

"Come on, Cindy—it's not a problem to be popular," Heather said at lunch that day. Cindy had just joined her friend at a table and filled her in on Max's startling invitation. "Aren't you flattered that he wants to go to the dance with you?"

"I'd rather go with you," Cindy muttered. She dropped her head into her hands and pushed away her lunch bag.

"We went together all last year, and we kept wishing we had someone to dance with," Heather reminded her. "I mean, isn't it better to go with someone like Max than just anybody? You know him really well—it won't be so embarrassing."

"I don't think I do know him well anymore. Everything's so different. We're starting high school; Max asked me out." Cindy blushed. "But I haven't changed, Heather. I like Max, but not as a boyfriend."

"So are you going to tell him you won't go to the dance with him?" Heather asked, biting into a peach.

Cindy thought it over. "I guess not," she finally said. "But what if he gets the wrong impression?"

"He won't." Heather shrugged. "Not unless you give it to him."

"I'll try not to." Cindy reached for her lunch, determined not to let what had happened with Max upset her.

But for the rest of the day she felt awkward every time she bumped into Max in the halls and when she sat behind him in her English class that afternoon. By the end of the school day Cindy was relieved that she had only one class with him. She couldn't help feeling disappointed. Before this morning, she had hoped they'd have a lot of classes together.

"I'm glad it's time to go home," Cindy said as she sat on the school bus with Heather. "I don't want to see Max anymore!"

"You can't avoid him for three weeks until the dance," Heather reminded her.

"No, but I wish I could." Cindy just couldn't picture herself as Max's girlfriend. Some of the girls at school had boyfriends, and they acted silly about it. The girls held hands with their boyfriends in the hallways and gossiped about them in class.

Frowning, Cindy glanced out the bus window. The early September day was fresh and clear, with a few clean-edged white clouds dotting the sky. She and Samantha had planned a trail ride when Cindy got home, and it looked like a perfect day for it. *I just won't worry about Max anymore*, Cindy told herself. *I'll take Glory out on the trails when I get home and enjoy myself. Horses are easier to understand than boys anyway. Well, except for Champion.*

*   *   *

"Okay, Cindy, I'd like to see a workout with Champion this morning," Ashleigh said early the next morning. "Work him three furlongs after you warm him up. I know it's only four days since he raced, but I'm not going to take it easy with him."

Cindy nodded as she tightened her helmet strap. "Do you hear that, Champion?" she asked. "Ashleigh's giving us no mercy. We've got a job to do. Cindy leaned forward to pat the colt's shoulder. His short, thick coat was sleek and glossy. Mornings Cindy could get him clean in no time. *He's a wash-and-wear horse*, she thought. *I wish everything were as easy with him.*

The colt pranced through the gap, his hooves barely touching the ground. The dawn sky was pale gray, with the barest pink touching the bottom of the clouds. The air was cool and damp from the storm the night before. The track was moist, but Cindy wasn't worried about it. Champion handled any surface well, at least in workouts. But he had never raced in mud.

He seems tense, Cindy thought, watching the colt's rigid neck and bunching shoulder muscles. She couldn't see any reason that he would be except that Limitless Time and Freedom's Ring were jogging slowly around the track in front of them. Samantha was up on Limitless Time, and a new exercise rider, Philip Marshall, was taking Freedom's Ring around.

"What's the problem, Champion?" Cindy asked. "You've seen those colts about a hundred times before."

Champion tossed his head and blew out a sharp snort. Cindy studied him for a moment, trying to figure out what he was thinking. An image of his last race flashed into her mind—of Champion almost knocking over Cajun King on his way to victory.

"I think I'll keep you away from the other colts today," she said. "I have a bad feeling about you, Champion. I think you learned something from your last race, but I'm not sure it was what we wanted you to learn at all."

Cindy sighed, thinking about the wonderful trail ride she'd had with Glory yesterday. The wind had been blowing hard, and she had felt as if it were lifting them up. Glory had gone so smoothly, he'd almost been flying.

Champion hauled on the reins, bringing her thoughts quickly back to him. *I'd better not daydream!* she realized, looking down at the colt. "Show me something good today, Champion," she said aloud.

Cindy trotted Champion around the track once. She could tell from the bunched muscles in Champion's neck that he yearned to gallop, but she wanted to be sure he was minding first.

Part of the problem is just that Champion is young, Cindy reminded herself. Glory had already been

101

three when she'd started working with him. Storm had been just two, like Champion, but Storm was the sweetest horse Cindy had ever known. Champion sometimes acted like a monster, but she realized his behavior was probably more typical of two-year-olds.

Cindy stopped the colt at the gap and looked at Ashleigh for instructions.

"Here come Limitless and Freedom," Ashleigh said. "Let's work Champion with them for three-eighths of a mile. I mentioned to Samantha and Philip that we'd probably work the colts together today."

I wonder if I should tell Ashleigh I don't think that's a good idea, Cindy thought. But she didn't want to second-guess Ashleigh.

Ashleigh seemed to understand. "I know it's a risk, Cindy, but Champion's a racehorse. He's never going to be running around the track by himself in a race. We have to get him used to racing with other horses."

"That's true." Cindy hesitated, trying to think how she should handle Champion if he chased the other colts. Samantha rode up on Limitless Time, stopping the bay colt a safe distance from Champion.

"If you're afraid, Cindy, someone else will take Champion around," Samantha said gently. "I'm not trying to insult you, but he ran a wild race on Saturday."

"No, it's okay. I'm not afraid." Cindy really wasn't, but she could understand how someone could think she might be. She sometimes wondered herself why she wasn't afraid of the colt. Champion had certainly proved that he could hurt people.

I guess I just think it'll be worth it in the end, she thought.

"Let's go, then," Samantha said. Cindy thought her older sister looked worried.

"Okay, Champion, keep your distance," Cindy warned as the powerful colt strained against the reins, trying to follow the other horses. "We want to win—but the right way, not by mowing anyone over."

Philip dropped back next to them on Freedom's Ring. Cindy had noticed when she was introduced to Philip that he was about twenty. This was his first job as an exercise rider. "I watched you take Champion around at a slow gallop yesterday," Philip said. "He's a handful, isn't he?"

"Sometimes," Cindy said. She was carefully watching Champion to see how he was reacting to Freedom. But Champion was ignoring the black colt. He was trotting in a perfect arc around the track.

Samantha lifted her hand and pointed forward, signaling a gallop. Cindy crouched over Champion's neck, asking for more speed. The colt had been galloped dozens of times before, and today he seemed to know what to do. He stayed at the steady, rocking pace Cindy asked for, just behind the other colts.

They were coming up on the three-eighths pole, where they would begin the work. Cindy could feel Champion tensing, probably in response to her own subtle get-ready signals.

"Now, boy!" she cried. Champion leaped forward, changing leads as he reached into a glorious run. Cindy went with him, her hands relaxed and steady over his neck, her body closely molded to his neck. Champion moved up to the outside of Limitless Time and Freedom.

"This is the life!" Samantha called.

"You bet!" Cindy grinned. Champion was running beautifully, neck and neck with Limitless and just behind Freedom.

The sun burst into view, a ball of brilliant orange light surrounded by fiery pink clouds. At almost the same instant Champion soared ahead. Cindy was thrown backward by the sudden rush of speed as Champion began to pull away from Limitless Time. "Yes!" Cindy cried breathlessly. Champion was going into his superdrive again! What kind of gallop was that? Whatever it was, she didn't want Champion to stop. "This is wonderful, boy!"

Suddenly Cindy saw that Freedom's Ring was bearing out. Philip was trying to block Champion's move on the outside to the lead. A couple of clods of loose dirt flew backward, striking Champion in the face.

Champion's ears pricked. With a surprised snort he increased his pace, coming up on Freedom's flank on the outside. "Watch out, Philip!" Cindy called. "You're in our way!"

"I'm trying to straighten him out!" Philip shouted. But Cindy saw that Freedom was too much for him. He was still drifting right into Champion's path. *I have to get Champion by,* Cindy thought. *We can't run into Freedom at this speed!*

Fighting his rider, Freedom inched closer to them. The black colt was so close, Cindy could feel the heat from his skin. Champion pulled against the left rein, turning to the other colt. In another second Cindy was sure Champion would lunge at Freedom!

With every ounce of riding skill that she possessed, Cindy pushed Champion forward with her hands and legs, crouching flat out over his neck as she asked him to drive by the other colt. *He's responding,* she realized with relief. *He's not going fast like he was, but he's still beating out Freedom.* Champion edged by the other colt and broke into the clear. Now Cindy only prayed that Freedom wouldn't run into the rail because of Champion's intimidation.

A glance over her shoulder reassured her that Philip had straightened out the other colt. *We're going to win this, whatever it is,* Cindy thought. *It's more like a boxing match than a workout!*

"Sorry," Philip yelled from behind her.

"It's okay." Cindy tried to keep Champion at a steady gallop. But the colt was upset, and he would hardly keep to a straight line. Cindy had no intention of trying him at a faster pace. The work was over.

"That was close," Samantha said as they stopped the horses at the gap.

"I know." Cindy swung out of the saddle. She expected Champion to jump sideways, and he did. Cindy expertly landed on her feet.

"Sorry, Cindy," Philip said sheepishly.

"It's all right." Cindy's breathing had almost returned to normal. "Nothing happened to the horses."

Ashleigh was shaking her head. "I know," Cindy said. "That was almost a disaster." Unrepentant, Champion was nudging her, as if to say would she please hand over the carrots he always got after his exercise.

"Let's take him down to the barn and talk about it," Ashleigh suggested.

"Okay." Ashleigh turned and started down the path. Cindy looked at Champion. "Did you really run as fast as I think you did?" she asked.

Champion bobbed his head and backed away from her. *I really may have just imagined it,* she thought.

Cindy hurried to catch up with Ashleigh. Champion

trotted behind, still grabbing at Cindy's pockets for carrots. "Ashleigh . . ." Cindy hesitated. She wanted to ask Ashleigh if she had noticed Champion's extra burst of speed, almost as if he had a superdrive gear. But she knew what she was about to say might sound completely dumb, especially after the bad performance Champion had just put in.

"What, Cindy?" Ashleigh stopped walking and smiled encouragingly.

Ashleigh always listens, no matter what I say, Cindy thought gratefully. "Did you notice that a little while after Champion changed leads in the stretch, he went even faster? It was almost like he was changing leads again."

"But he didn't." Ashleigh nodded. "Yes, I noticed. Townsend Victory may have been able to do that, too. Recently I was watching some videos of his races. In his last race, the one that he broke down in, he had switched leads in the stretch. Then, for a couple of strides right near the wire it looked like he had picked up the pace—again. A second later he lunged at that other colt and injured himself. I don't know if we can ever be sure."

"Sounds like Champion." Cindy winced. "Both the speed *and* going out of control."

"What he's doing out there is serious," Ashleigh said. "Maybe Champion can overpower his rivals no matter how much he acts up. But I don't like it, Cindy. He could get beaten—or hurt."

I don't know what else to try with him, Cindy thought, biting her lip. But she had to agree with Ashleigh—they were running out of time.

"Now you're being nice," Cindy said to Champion that afternoon as she rode him at a walk across the flower-filled meadow where Storm was buried.

"He almost never spooks," Samantha agreed. She was riding Limitless Time. "That's rare for a young horse."

"Champion's smart, all right." Cindy stopped the colt in front of Storm's grave and dismounted.

"Maybe Champion likes trail rides better than the track," Samantha suggested. Cindy had noticed that during the whole ride to the meadow, Champion had walked and trotted next to Limitless without any trouble at all. He seemed to like the bay colt better than Freedom. *Just another one of Champion's preferences*, she thought.

"I think he likes the track, too," Cindy said. She dismounted at Storm's grave and bent to examine the flowers. "He doesn't act sour out there." Cindy carefully snipped a few dead blossoms from the flowers with a pair of clippers she had brought.

"You still come here a lot, don't you?" Samantha asked, looking at the neat grave.

"Sometimes." Cindy hoped Samantha wouldn't tell her that she should be over her grief for Storm by now. Cindy knew she still needed to come here. Champion's work this morning had been so difficult. Her second day of high school, coming right after it, had left her feeling confused and stressed. She still had to struggle to find her way around, and trying to act normal toward Max now was almost unbearable. In the quiet and beauty of Storm's meadow, close to her beloved horse, Cindy felt quiet stealing into her soul.

"Don't worry—I think I understand how you feel," Samantha said. She dismounted from Limitless Time and came over to stand beside Cindy. "You never get over some things," she said slowly.

"Like what else?" Cindy asked, smelling the flowers deeply.

"Like my mother's death." Samantha sighed.

"Yeah, I guess you never would." Cindy looked at Samantha sympathetically. Samantha's mother had died in a riding accident when Samantha was twelve. She had been very close to her mother, and her sudden death had left Samantha severely traumatized. Cindy's parents had died in a car crash when she was a baby, but she had no memory of them.

"Cindy, you have to try to go on," Samantha continued. "I love Beth now. That doesn't mean I've forgotten my own mother or that the pain of losing her isn't still there. But I've let myself be open to new love."

"That makes sense," Cindy said. She knew that it did, but she still couldn't *feel* that it did.

Samantha nodded. "You may just need a little more time."

Champion had moved closer to the grave and was nibbling one of Storm's flowers. "Stop it!" Cindy said, torn between amusement and tears. Champion was comically holding a daisy in his mouth and backing off.

"He's just enjoying the flowers in his own way," Samantha said with a laugh. "Champion's really a good horse, Cindy."

"I think so, too." Cindy held out her hand. "Come here. I'm not going to take your flower away." Champion stepped closer to her, his expression still guarded.

"Should we head on?" Samantha asked. "I don't want to rush you."

"That's okay." Cindy looked at the grave. So much of her heart seemed to be buried with Storm. She wondered if she would ever get it back. "I can come another time."

10

THAT NIGHT CINDY SLIPPED OUT OF THE COTTAGE AND walked to the mares' barn to visit Wonder. Cindy had finished her homework, but she couldn't stop thinking about Max. Cindy had tried to avoid him all day. She had ducked into the girls' bathroom whenever she saw him and run down the halls to her classes so that they wouldn't have a chance to talk. Cindy knew she was going to explode if she had to go through another day like that. Seeing Wonder would remind her of the familiar, good things in life, she thought.

The night was thick and still. The heavy air made everything smell sweet and luscious. Cindy could feel herself relaxing. *It's still really summer*, she thought. *And I have three weeks till the dance and Champion's next race. There's still time to figure things out with Champion and Max.*

As Cindy walked down the aisle in the mares' barn she saw Ashleigh standing in front of Princess's and Honor's stalls and heard Ashleigh's soft voice. "So are you a pretty girl? You're the prettiest there ever was, except for your mother."

Cindy smiled. Ashleigh sounded like she was having a conversation with a person. "Hi, Ashleigh," she said.

"Oh, hi, Cindy." Ashleigh turned and smiled. "Are you here to see Honor and Princess, too?"

"Kind of. I really wanted to see Wonder." Wonder's stall was right next to Princess's.

Ashleigh nodded. "I can understand that. But is there any particular reason you want to see Wonder at eleven o'clock at night?"

Cindy hesitated. She felt shy about sharing her problems with Ashleigh.

"Sit," Ashleigh said, pointing at a hay bale in front of Wonder's stall. "Tell me what's wrong."

Cindy heard a rustle, and Wonder looked out of her stall. Wonder's eyes were soft in her beautiful face, as if she knew Cindy had a problem and sympathized.

"Is high school a bit much for you?" Ashleigh asked. "Do you have a lot more homework?"

"Not really. I don't usually have a problem with schoolwork." Cindy hesitated. *Remember you can tell Ashleigh anything*, she thought. *All right—here goes.*

"It's about Max," she said. "You know we've been friends for years."

Ashleigh nodded. "Old friends are the best. I've still got a few from when I was your age."

"But I don't think Max is my friend anymore." Cindy felt her cheeks reddening.

"Did you have a fight?" Ashleigh asked, her voice kind.

"No, not at all. Max asked me to a dance! And the way he was acting . . ." Cindy sighed deeply. "I think he likes me as a girlfriend instead of just as a friend."

"Sounds like it," Ashleigh agreed. "Do you want to go to the dance?"

"Kind of. But not if it's going to be totally embarrassing." Cindy dropped her head into her hands.

"Just take it slow," Ashleigh advised. "Why don't you try going to this one dance with Max? If you don't like it and it makes you feel uncomfortable, don't go to another one. But I think before you go, you need to talk to him and clear up any misunderstanding."

"That sounds good." Cindy could feel her mood lightening. She'd always been able to talk to Max— why wouldn't she be able to now? "Thanks for not laughing at me," Cindy murmured. "I know this is kind of a dumb problem."

"Believe me, I wouldn't laugh at you," Ashleigh said. "You're doing better than I did in ninth grade. I

113

must have been the most awkward kid in school when I was your age."

"Really?" Cindy couldn't imagine that. Ashleigh always seemed so poised.

"Really," Ashleigh confirmed. "My best friend, Linda March, said I used to scowl at the boys so much, they were all afraid to dance with me. I think she was right."

"It'll feel good to talk to Max about this and get it off my mind," Cindy said. She reached up to stroke Wonder's velvet muzzle, and the mare gratefully bent her head to accept the caress. Cindy thought Wonder looked a little lonely without a foal. "Who are you going to breed her to next year?" she asked.

"I haven't decided, but we've got a lot of time. I owe it to Wonder to find a special stallion for her." Ashleigh smiled. "Wonder's one of those friends I've kept for a long time. I hope she'll have many more great sons and daughters."

"How's Mr. Wonderful doing?" Cindy asked. She knew that Ashleigh had put the colt out to pasture for a rest as soon as he returned from Del Mar. He looked as exquisitely beautiful as ever to Cindy, but he couldn't seem to gain back the weight he had lost after the race. Cindy hoped the colt was at last showing signs of returning to his old self.

Ashleigh's smile disappeared. "I'm worried about him," she said grimly. "He's still missing his vital spark."

"Has Dr. Smith been back out to check him?" Cindy asked.

Ashleigh nodded. "She still can't find anything wrong. But we'll get to the bottom of it, Cindy."

I sure hope so, Cindy thought. *Because I don't think Ashleigh can really be happy until we do.*

"Why are you just standing by the door?" Heather asked Cindy the next day after Cindy's English class.

"Waiting for Max—I've got to talk to him about the dance," Cindy whispered. Other students in the class were crowding out the door, and Cindy felt painfully conspicuous. All she needed was for everyone to guess what she was doing.

"Hey, Cindy," Melissa Souter called. Melissa's father owned a Thoroughbred training and breeding farm. She and her friends Laura Billings and Sharon Rodgers often ate lunch with Cindy and Heather.

"Hi." Cindy hoped Melissa wouldn't come over and start a conversation. As far as she knew, Max hadn't told anyone that he had asked her to the dance. Cindy didn't want everyone to find out, especially since she wasn't even sure if she and Max were going.

Heather seemed to understand. "Hey, you guys," she said, walking quickly over to Melissa and her friends. "Did you understand the homework assignment?" Heather looked back at Cindy and winked.

Cindy was too upset to wink back. Her throat was suddenly so dry, she could hardly swallow. *This is serious*, she realized. *Max is one of my very best friends.* He was the kind of friend that Cindy had hoped to keep forever, like Ashleigh had said. *I hope he doesn't take this wrong*, she thought.

"Are you waiting for me?" Max was standing beside her, holding his books under his arm.

"Yes, I was." Cindy plunged ahead before she lost her nerve. "Max, I'm just not too sure about going to the dance."

Max frowned. "Why not?" he asked. "You said you would."

"But that was before . . ." Cindy trailed off lamely. *It's one thing to talk about horses with Max and another to talk with him about being his girlfriend*, she thought. *This isn't going to be easy!*

"Before what?" Max asked impatiently.

"Before I realized that you might not think about it the way I do," Cindy blurted. *What is the matter with me?* she thought in dismay. *I'm not saying this right at all!*

Max stared at her in astonishment. "What are you talking about?" he asked.

"Nothing." Cindy shrugged. "Just forget it." She didn't know what to say next. Her cheeks were burning, and she couldn't look Max in the eye.

"No, you forget it," Max said angrily. "Let's not go

to the dance. I don't care anyhow." He stomped off down the hall, leaving Cindy staring after him openmouthed.

"I sure blew that," she murmured. "Now how will Max and I ever be friends again?"

That evening Cindy walked out to see Storm. Since her fight with Max she'd had so much excess energy, she had to let it out somehow. Cindy hadn't brought Champion, the way she usually did. The colt's high spirits and pushiness weren't what she was in the mood for right now. This morning she had only walked him because he had been thoroughly exercised the day before, during the wild ride with Limitless and Freedom. But even at a snail's pace Champion hadn't given her an easy time of it.

I do come out here to see Storm a lot, Cindy thought guiltily as she neared the neat dirt mound of Storm's grave. *But I really have to tonight. So much is going wrong!*

Cindy looked around to see if anyone was watching her. But she was completely alone except for an owl, hooting softly in the nearby woods. The warm blue twilight turned the trees and the grass of the meadow blue as night fell at Whitebrook.

"It's so nice here," Cindy murmured as she sat down among the daisies, black-eyed Susans, and tiger lilies that edged Storm's grave. She could feel herself starting to relax. At the edge of the forest a doe and her fawn cautiously stepped into the meadow to graze.

"I guess I've got a lot of problems, but they don't seem so bad when I'm out here," Cindy said aloud. "Max is a problem—I don't think you can help me much with him, Storm." Cindy sighed, remembering her last conversation with Max. "But what about Champion? Why does he act up so much?"

Cindy felt strangely comforted as she sat beside the grave and told her horse her troubles. She knew there weren't really answers here, but she always found peace.

I think Storm's spirit is close to me, she thought. *I feel like he understands*.

"You were so sweet and gentle, Storm." Cindy bowed her head. "I know you'd tell me what to do with Champion if you could. I wish you'd been stronger and lived. But you had so much heart—you were strong that way. Champion's incredibly talented, but I just don't think he has as much heart as you did. I don't think there'll ever be a horse like you again, boy," she said sadly.

Cindy almost cried out as a whirlwind of bats swept out of a nearby tree. The bats were black against the darkening sky. Cindy shivered as the damp, earthy-smelling scent of night crept over the meadow. "I'm so lonesome for you, Storm," she whispered.

11

THREE WEEKS LATER CINDY WINCED AS LIGHTNING cracked across the sky at the Turfway Park track. It was the day of the Kentucky Cup Juvenile Stakes, Champion's third race in the Bonus Series. The late September weather had been stormy most of the week.

Thunder boomed directly overhead. *Today is the worst weather yet*, Cindy thought.

Champion's ears shot up at the sound. The colt shook himself, making raindrops fly from his wet coat, almost black from the moisture. Ian and Mike had kept Champion sheeted until a minute ago, but it was almost post time. Ashleigh stood at the edge of the walking ring, ready to mount. Her blue-and-white racing silks were already darkened by rain.

"Steady, Champion," Cindy said, stepping closer

119

to the colt's head. She didn't like the look in Champion's eyes. Lightning flashed again and the colt half reared, silhouetted against the bright sky. *He looks like a wild stallion!* Cindy thought. She clung to Champion's reins, willing him not to go over on his back. Champion came down on four feet again, but Cindy could see the whites of his eyes as he glanced around. He wasn't calming down.

"Don't run your race on the backside, Champion," Ashleigh said. Her voice was assured as always, but Cindy saw lines of tension in the young jockey's face.

Cindy put a soothing hand on Champion's wet neck. "It's okay, boy," she said. "You don't really mind the rain, do you?"

Champion looked back at Cindy, his gaze alert but soft. For a moment his ears relaxed. But in a second he pricked them again and twisted his head abruptly to stare at the walking ring. The other horses in the field were just entering the ring from the saddling paddock.

The colt shivered from head to toe. "Don't be nervous," Cindy pleaded. But Champion seemed not to hear her. He danced in place, churning the soggy ground under his feet. The muscles in his powerful shoulders and hindquarters were sharply defined under his slick coat. He looked as perfectly sculpted as a statue and gloriously beautiful. *He can win this race*, Cindy thought. *If he'll just mind Ashleigh!*

Secret Sign, a Kentucky bred just coming off a win in an allowance race at Turfway, whinnied loudly from the walking ring and tried to pull away from his handler. Secret Sign looked black in the rain, but Cindy could see from his dry underside that he was gray. *All the other horses are just as young and bothered by the weather as Champion is,* she told herself. *I just hope they don't bother each other.*

"The track's listed as muddy." Ian checked the colt's girth for the last time.

"I'm not sure how any of the horses are going to take to this surface." Ashleigh frowned as she adjusted her stirrups. "A couple of the jockeys have said they don't even want to ride when the track is such a mess."

"So far three horses have been scratched," Ian said. "That still leaves an eight-horse field. Are you sure you want to ride, Ashleigh?"

Ashleigh nodded firmly and took up on Champion's reins. "Wow, the reins are already slippery!"

"I think we're about to find out how Champion handles mud in his face," Mike said anxiously. "He's almost sure to take some, since he's breaking from the five hole."

Cindy remembered with a sinking feeling that Champion hadn't liked being hit with dirt on the Whitebrook track. *But maybe Ashleigh can take*

Champion right to the front and keep him there, she thought. *I sure hope he wins—I'm ready for a change of luck!*

The past three weeks had been a nightmare for Cindy. After her painful fight with Max, she hadn't spoken to him again. In the halls at school and in class she'd noticed that he was avoiding her. Cindy could hardly believe that their friendship was over so fast.

"Champion's had mud in his face before, but nothing like this," Ashleigh said. "We'll just have to see how he reacts."

Cindy nodded, though she felt anything but confident. For weeks Champion had continued to be unpredictable in his workouts, even when he wasn't challenged by bad weather and a muddy track. Cindy knew that Ashleigh had almost scratched him from today's race after his last work at Turfway, three days ago. Champion had chased a claimer halfway around the track.

As if all that weren't enough bad news, Mr. Wonderful still wasn't up to form. Ashleigh, Ian, and Mike had no plans for his comeback on the track.

"I'll see how quickly I can get Champion to the front," Ashleigh said.

"You may not have much choice about where he runs on a day like this," Ian said. "Probably no horse will be running his usual race in this slop."

"Except possibly for Secret Sign," Ashleigh said. "It's early in his career to tell, but he's won a couple of races in the mud."

"Secret Sign sounds like an emerging mudder." Mike rested a hand on one of Ashleigh's boots and looked up at her. Ashleigh smiled and reached down to hold his hand.

From the walking ring Secret Sign whinnied sharply. Champion twisted his head and whinnied back. *Uh-oh*, Cindy thought. *I wonder what they're saying?* She hoped Champion would leave the other horses alone on the track and concentrate on running.

"Secret Sign is nice looking, huh?" Ashleigh said.

Cindy nodded. Secret Sign was well muscled and perfectly correct, as far as she could see. She knew that a lot of the press's attention was focused on the gray colt as a rising star.

"You've got all your goggles?" Mike asked Ashleigh.

Ashleigh held them up. Cindy knew that Ashleigh would have half a dozen pairs of goggles. When one pair got dirty with mud thrown up from the track, Ashleigh would toss it off and pull down another pair.

I think she's going to need a lot of sets today! Cindy thought.

"Get through the race in one piece," Mike said softly. "It's going to be wild out there."

"I will." Ashleigh gave him a confident smile. "Now I'd better go. Here comes the rest of the field."

"Good luck." Mike patted Champion's neck.

"I'll definitely need it today." Ashleigh touched her helmet with her crop. "See you guys later."

Cindy saw Champion try to twist his head around for one last look at the other horses, but Ashleigh kept him going with her hands and heels. *Ashleigh will get him through the race*, Cindy thought. *That is, if anyone can.* She sighed. There had to be some way to do better than just get Champion through races. He wasn't supposed to just survive out there, but run his fastest.

The rain had been coming down in sheets all morning. Now it had let up a little, but Cindy's blond hair was soaked. Big drops ran into her eyes.

"I think the weather is clearing," Ian remarked as they walked to the stands.

"Good," Mike said tersely. "Electrical storms drive some horses crazy."

"I noticed that storms get on Champion's nerves," Cindy said. "Why is that?"

"I think some horses are extremely sensitive to electricity in the air." Mike shrugged. "But Champion's not the worst I've seen."

Cindy walked backward to check out the sky. In the west the clouds were breaking up into puffs of light and dark gray. Cindy sniffed the sharp, clean smell of ozone left over from the storm.

"Champion's behavior is bad enough without the weather making it worse," Ian said. "When I spoke to the stewards, they agreed to let us take Champion out by himself, but they made it clear that this is the last time. Other owners and trainers want to know why he gets special treatment. They'd like the same for their horses."

"But the last race in the Bonus Series, the Breeders' Futurity, is at Keeneland, not here." Cindy glanced at her dad. "So it'll be different stewards deciding what to do with Champion, right?"

"No, it's the same ones, Cindy." Mike said.

"Great." Cindy caught a glimpse of Sandsation, a West Coast colt, just leaving the walking ring. Checking the board, she saw that he was going in as the third choice after Secret Sign and Champion. Cindy remembered that the bay colt was coming off a win in a nonwinners-of-two race at Belmont and was known for early speed. But like Champion, he would be running for the first time around two turns.

Sandsation may burn out at a mile and a sixteenth, Cindy thought as she sat next to Beth in the stands. *This really may be Champion's race.* At least nobody doubted that Champion was strong.

"How come Champion isn't going into the race as

125

the favorite?" she asked her dad. "He won the Bashford and Juvenile Stakes."

"Yes, but by the skin of his teeth." Ian shook his head. "He was almost out of control in both races. Secret Sign's performances have been much more consistent."

Samantha smiled reassuringly at Cindy, and Beth took her hand. But Cindy felt far from reassured.

The horses were loading in the gate. Cindy saw Champion balk as an attendant tried to lead him into the five slot. "Don't start already, Champion!" Cindy muttered. Before Champion had time to think about acting up more, four burly gate attendants had pushed and pulled him inside.

"Good," Mike said. "Maybe Champion's gotten that out of his system."

Cindy doubted it. The next second she saw for sure that Mike was wrong. Champion was just warming up! "He's rearing in the gate!" Cindy's hands flew to her mouth. She had an awful sense of déjà vu. Champion was behaving just as badly in the gate as he had in the Bashford Stakes.

Champion went higher, clawing the sky. "Ashleigh's slipping off backward!" Samantha cried.

Champion's going to go over on Ashleigh! Cindy screamed silently. That could kill her!

Miraculously Ashleigh clung to the colt's back, her hands wrapped in his mane. Champion slowly low-

126

ered to the ground. The next second the gate flipped open, and eight Thoroughbreds lunged forward, churning up a great curtain of mud.

"Ashleigh's okay!" Mike said. "But Champion's off a beat slow."

Cindy tried to identify the horses. Already they were covered with mud and a uniform gray-brown. Suddenly she picked out Champion at the edge of the pack, fighting for traction. The colt slipped to the inside, almost bumping Secret Sign. The gray colt slid inside also.

"Here we go again!" Samantha cried. "Another disaster with Champion on the track. I can't believe Ashleigh didn't fall off in the gate!"

"At least Secret Sign didn't hit anyone," Beth said. "The rest of the field is already down the track."

That's the problem! Cindy clenched her hands into fists. *But Ashleigh and Champion pulled it out in the Bashford and Juvenile Stakes,* she reminded herself. Frantically she scanned the track, trying to see the horses' positions through the mud as they whipped into the clubhouse turn. "Champion's dead last!" she said in dismay.

"He broke badly from the gate and then slipped— it's not surprising." Ian raised his binoculars as the horses surged around the first turn.

"Thank goodness Ashleigh stayed with him," Mike said. Cindy had never seen him look so wor-

127

ried. She couldn't blame him. Ashleigh had already had several close calls, and the race was barely under way.

The horses splattered into the backstretch. "It's Sandsation on the lead, with Ruby's Slipper and Sky Dancer up close second," the announcer called. "Nefarious in third, followed by Tap to the Music and Closet Affair. Secret Sign and Wonder's Champion are trailing the pack." To her horror, Cindy saw that Champion and Secret Sign were engaged in a private match race—but about ten lengths behind the leaders! Champion was running just outside Secret Sign, his head at the other colt's flank.

"Can Champion make up enough ground to win?" Cindy turned quickly to her dad.

"It's unlikely," Ian called over the crowd noise.

Cindy slumped in her seat. She wondered dismally if one of Wonder's offspring had ever been so far behind in a race. Champion seemed fully extended, his long legs reaching for ground.

With a glimmer of hope Cindy remembered Champion's superdrive. *He might have more*, she thought. *He could still kick in—they've got half a mile to go!*

The clouds had swept in again, darkening the day. Cindy wiped a fine mist from her face and peered at the track. Eight gleaming bodies drove furiously through the soggy surface, blurred by drizzle and mud. Champion and Secret Sign were still in last place, battling it out as they drove around the far turn. "Come on, Champion," Cindy said under her breath. "It's now or never!"

As if he had finally had enough of being last, Champion burst ahead of Secret Sign coming into the stretch. The horses were approaching the stands, and Cindy could see better.

"Champion can't get up in time," Ian said.

"But he can make a good showing," Cindy cried. "Please, Champion!"

The big colt seemed to have heard. With a bound he surged ahead, almost clearing Secret Sign. *There he goes!* Cindy thought excitedly. *He's in superdrive!*

Suddenly Champion bore in sharply toward the rail. "What happened?" Samantha gasped.

"I'm not sure," Ian said, half rising from his seat. "He may have stumbled or slipped."

"It's too late to matter." Cindy almost sobbed. The horses swept under the wire, with Sky Dancer ahead of the pack by a length and Champion next to last. *Champion's just lost his chance to sweep the Bonus series*, she thought. *And that's not all—I don't know if Dad or Mike will ever have confidence in him again.*

"This is a disaster." Ian groaned.

"Let's see how Ashleigh and Champion are doing." Mike got up and led the way out of the stands to the track.

Ashleigh had already dismounted by the time the Whitebrook group reached her. Cindy tried to see Champion as she struggled through the crowd. The colt was blowing hard and caked with mud, but he didn't seem to be in distress, she noted with relief.

Champion spotted her and raised his head. He whickered a greeting with his usual self-possession and took a step toward her.

"What kind of ride do you call that?" Secret Sign's jockey, Shawn Biermont, yelled at Ashleigh.

"Hey, leave her alone," Mike said, shouldering his way through the onlookers to reach Ashleigh's side.

"I didn't have much choice today about where my colt ran, Shawn." Ashleigh sounded tired. She wiped mud off her forehead. "And I really think it was pointless for you to whip my horse."

"Whip him!" Cindy gasped. That was why Champion had jumped sideways in the stretch. "Is he okay?"

"I don't think it left a mark, but if Champion had fallen at that speed, he and I both could have been badly injured or killed." Ashleigh looked straight at Shawn.

"Your ill-mannered colt goes after other horses in every race. I was just trying to get him away from Secret Sign!" Shawn shouted.

"Oh, come on. We both know perfectly well that's not true." Ashleigh shrugged and turned away.

130

Cindy saw a well-dressed man shaking his fist at Ashleigh. Secret Sign's owner, Cindy presumed.

"Come on, Ashleigh," Mike said, protectively putting an arm around her shoulders. "Let's get out of here."

Champion repeatedly nudged Cindy, as if he had something to say. "Champion, I don't know what to do with you," Cindy said with a heavy sigh. "What on earth were you doing out there?"

Cindy noticed that a couple of reporters were looking at Champion with scornful expressions. "So what do you think of your wonder horse now?" one reporter asked Ashleigh.

"I don't think mud is his favorite surface." Ashleigh shook her head.

"He can't load in the gate or break properly, and he just about killed Secret Sign out there," the reporter added. "I don't know what you're doing even running him."

Cindy was almost sick with disappointment. She couldn't stand the reporter's sneering tone. Obviously he hadn't seen Shawn whip Champion, either.

"There are two sides to every story," Ashleigh said.

The reporter turned to Cindy. "You're Wonder's Champion's exercise rider, aren't you?" he asked abruptly. "What do you think of your horse's future after his performance today?"

131

"I think he's going to win the Kentucky Derby next year," Cindy said hotly.

The reporters laughed loudly. Cindy's cheeks burned despite the cool rain. She couldn't bear to hear them laugh at her horse.

"Cindy." Ashleigh touched her elbow. "Let's go. Champion needs you."

Cindy took a deep breath and turned back to Champion. She knew that Ashleigh was right. *I shouldn't care what they think*, she thought. *I know they're wrong about Champion*. The colt was looking at her hopefully, still blowing hard from his effort. He seemed to be wondering if she was mad at him. "Oh, of course I still love you," Cindy said. "But you're in a lot of trouble."

"He sure is," Ian confirmed. "I was just told that Champion is on the gate list."

"Oh, no!" Cindy knew that being on the gate list meant that Champion couldn't race again until he had demonstrated in the gate, by himself, to the track officials' satisfaction that he had good gate manners.

"Well, I kind of agree with the criticism we're getting from all sides," Ashleigh said quietly as she, Cindy, Ian, and Mike led the colt toward the backside. "If we can't make Champion behave before a race or during it, we definitely need to make some changes."

"The last race in the Bonus Series is in just three

132

weeks," Cindy said. "Are you still going to enter Champion in it, Dad?"

Ian shook his head. "At this point I don't know, Cindy. I'd like to—but it depends on him. Today I'm not optimistic."

"It's hard to be right now," Mike said.

"If Champion hadn't been seventh, he certainly would have been placed lower than that for interference," Ashleigh said. "But Secret Sign wasn't running well, either. His jockey's and owner's comments are out of line—Champion didn't cost them anything."

"Of course not," Mike said consolingly.

"I'm going to get cleaned up." Ashleigh looked at Champion appraisingly. Then she turned to Cindy. "We've got a lot to talk about."

"I know," Cindy said unhappily. "Come on, Champion."

The colt braced his legs and shook himself, splattering raindrops and mud. Then he lifted his head and whinnied loudly.

Despite Champion's terrible performance in the race, Cindy couldn't help admiring the colt's looks. He held his exquisite head high, as if he had every reason to be proud.

Champion looks like a great racehorse, Cindy thought. *And I know he's got the talent to be one. It's just so frustrating not to be able to tap that talent.*

133

12

"LET'S START OVER WITH HIM," ASHLEIGH SAID THE NEXT day in the truck as she and Cindy vanned Champion back to Whitebrook. Mike and Ian had returned home from the track the previous day. Cindy had gladly agreed to accompany Ashleigh to bring the colt home. "We can't have Champion acting like he did in the first three races of the Bonus Series," Ashleigh added. "Especially the last one, obviously."

"I know," Cindy said glumly. She looked through the rear window to check on Champion. The colt was riding in Whitebrook's two-horse trailer by himself since none of the other horses from the farm had raced that weekend at Turfway. He was bouncing a little as the trailer hit uneven places in the road. But he was such a big colt, there wasn't much room for him to move in the trailer stall. Cindy noticed that

Champion had a dark eye fixed on her through the small tinted window of the trailer.

Cindy turned back around and blew out a breath. *That race was a nightmare from start to finish*, she thought. *I still can't believe Champion lost!*

"Champion's track habits are getting worse, not better," Ashleigh continued as she slowly made a turn, careful to let the colt shift his weight and find his balance. "I can't fool myself about that anymore. He's not going to grow out of it or snap out of it."

Cindy shook her head. "I don't think so, either."

"We need to correct him at every step of the way, from the stall to the track," Ashleigh said firmly. "We've overlooked a lot of his misbehavior because he's a strong, talented colt. Until the Kentucky Cup that was enough for him to win races. But it's not anymore. The first step is to get him ready to pass the gate test."

Cindy nodded. Until Champion passed the gate test, he couldn't race at all.

"Let's give him today to settle back in at home, then start first thing tomorrow morning with gate work," Ashleigh said.

"Sounds good," Cindy said with determination. She had been the first to work Champion in the gate that spring. Gate work would be a good starting point for Champion's retraining, she thought. It was something he had always done well for her.

Cindy felt a slight chill as she remembered how

badly Champion had behaved in the gate for Ashleigh in both the Bashford and yesterday's race. *What went wrong?* she wondered. *Will Champion rear up on me, too? Ashleigh's one of the best riders in the world. How will I be able to sit out Champion's rearing when Ashleigh barely could?*

"How's he doing?" Ashleigh asked.

"He seems fine." Cindy settled back into her seat. Outside, the weather had cleared. The sky was a startling robin's-egg blue, washed clean by the rain. *The track at home will be a little soggy tomorrow morning, but that shouldn't make much difference in Champion's retraining,* Cindy decided. *If he's impossible, a little mud won't change that.*

"Our plans for Champion seem good," Ashleigh said. She smiled encouragingly. "Let's not lose hope."

"I won't." Cindy looked back at the colt. The trailer swung around a curve and Champion lost his balance a little, but he was still watching her. "I just wonder what Champion's plans are," she said. She was sure the mischievous colt had his own.

Early the next morning Cindy walked down the path to the training barn. She smiled as she heard the eager stamp of the horses' hooves in the stalls. The horses in training had been fed already, and they were impatiently awaiting their riders and exercise sessions.

The morning was clear and almost calm. A faint

warm breeze barely lifted Cindy's hair and tickled her cheeks. Cindy sniffed the delicious summer smells of clover, flowers, and damp grass. The paddocks were already full of gorgeous Thoroughbred mares, foals, and stallions. Len and the other stable workers had put the horses out right after breakfast to let them bask in the sun and graze.

In the front paddock Honor Bright stood stock still, watching Cindy. Lucky Chance nipped the little bay filly, and both foals skyrocketed across the emerald grass, kicking up their heels with sheer joy. Cindy smiled, thoroughly enjoying the clean, perfect action of the young horses.

Someday I might be riding them! I can hardly wait till I'm sixteen and can get my apprentice jockey's license, she said to herself.

"Hi, Cindy!" Vic waved. He, Mark, and Philip were walking over to the training barn from Len's cottage. All four men were sharing the cottage while a new one was being constructed close by. Ian and Mike had apologized for crowding Len, but he said he enjoyed the company. Len hadn't had a roommate since Charlie Burke, Wonder's old trainer, had died.

Cindy waved back at the other exercise riders. "Great day, huh?" Philip asked.

"It sure is." Cindy hoped she and Champion would have a great day out on the track, too. They were due for one, she thought.

In the barn Len already had the colt in crossties. "Morning, Cindy," Len said, hanging Champion's bridle from a nail. "I brushed him for you."

"Thanks," Cindy said gratefully. Len often had Champion all ready for Cindy in the morning since on school days, she didn't have a lot of time. Cindy knew that in his quiet way Len was one of Champion's biggest fans. He helped her as much as he could.

Champion whinnied and pawed the aisle. Cindy couldn't help smiling at the sight of the beautiful colt. Champion's dark coat glowed, and his eyes were bright. He was clearly raring to get out there and begin another day.

"This is an important session, Champion," Cindy told the colt as she flipped a saddle pad onto his back. "We're going to get you into that gate. No more backsliding. You really don't have much further to slide."

Champion quickly twisted his head around as far as he could in the crossties to look at her. "Do you understand?" Cindy asked.

Champion bobbed his head energetically. Either he agreed with her or he was just interested in Limitless Time, who was leaving his stall two doors down with Samantha. "Okay, Champion, I'm going to take that as a yes," Cindy said. "So don't forget our agreement."

Cindy quickly finished tacking up the colt and double-checked their equipment. She anticipated a rough ride today. The last thing she needed was to have a saddle or bridle break or come loose.

"You mind Cindy this morning," Len told the colt, resting a hand on Champion's neck.

"He'd better." Cindy sighed as she led Champion to the door of the barn. "He's really starting to scare me, Len. I don't mean I'm scared to ride him. But he's almost out of chances."

"Well, be careful out there." Len patted Champion's neck. "Take care of her, big guy."

"I wish he would." For just a second Cindy remembered Storm's gentleness and the trust she'd had in him. Every training session had been pure joy, a time of oneness with her horse.

But Storm was gone. Cindy shook her head and led Champion out of the barn.

The colt willingly followed, almost walking up Cindy's heels. The ground squished a little under Champion's hooves, but he didn't seem to be having any trouble walking on the soft surface. "I don't think the footing will be a problem today," she told him. "I'll warm you up a little, but we're only going to walk into the gate. We're not going to fly around the track."

Champion pulled hard on the reins, as if to say that didn't suit him at all.

"I'm sorry, but you asked for it," Cindy said firmly. "You're in the doghouse with the track officials."

At the track Ashleigh, Ian, and Mike were waiting for them. "We're all going to watch Champion today," Ashleigh told Cindy. "Just to make sure we see from every angle what's going on with him."

"Sure." Cindy gulped. Champion was really under the gun now, she thought. Having such a critical audience was making her nervous.

Champion skittered sideways to the end of the reins. He seemed nervous as well. Then Cindy saw him looking at the practice gate, already set up on the inside of the track. *Uh-oh. He knows what's coming, and this is how he's acting. I'm not going to have an easy time.*

Ashleigh gave her a leg up into the saddle. "Take him around a couple of times to let him stretch his legs, then we'll try him in the gate. I have a feeling this is either going to be simple or a major problem."

Cindy nodded. Those did seem to be the two choices with Champion.

She drew a deep breath and tried to relax. To her left she could see Glory and Pride, each out in one of the stallion paddocks. Pride was grazing, but Glory was standing motionless, looking over the fence toward the training activities. The two powerful stallions sparkled copper and silver in the sunshine.

Cindy patted Champion's neck. "You're a lucky

guy—you get to go out on the track. I can tell Glory wishes he did."

Champion set off at a walk without being asked. "Okay." Cindy sighed, then smiled. Champion should have waited for her request to walk, but maybe she shouldn't fight him on every little thing. "I want to get going, too."

Cindy walked and trotted Champion around the track several times. The colt obeyed her easily, his long, silky dark mane and tail blowing in their own breeze.

"Okay, let's try him in the gate!" Ashleigh called as Cindy drew Champion up at the gap.

Cindy felt her muscles tense. It was hard not to be nervous about taking Champion in that small, enclosed space. A lot of accidents happened in the gate, and Champion had nearly flipped on Ashleigh the last time he'd been in one.

"Walk him in and out with the doors open," Ian said, his forehead furrowed with worry. "Cindy, I'd feel a lot better if one of the other riders took him in."

Cindy shook her head. "I think he'll be okay." She wasn't sure of that, but she was sure that Champion would act up worse for anyone else.

The colt's ears pricked as she pointed him toward the gate, but he steadily walked up to it and on through. Cindy let out the breath she hadn't realized she was holding. The next time Champion calmly stood in the gate while Ashleigh shut the front and back gates.

"And that's that," Ian said, sounding relieved. Ashleigh opened the gates, and Cindy walked Champion out.

"Once more," Ashleigh said.

Glory whinnied loudly from his paddock. Cindy glanced over and saw the gray stallion still waiting by the fence, hanging his head longingly over the top board.

Champion whinnied back. "Now you've told Glory hello," Cindy said. "But we've got work to do here, Champion." She urged him forward with her legs.

The colt remained frozen, staring at Glory.

"Come on, Champion." Ian reached for the colt's reins.

Champion trembled from head to foot. His forelegs lifted slightly. "Watch out," Cindy cried. "He's going up!"

That was the wrong thing to say! she realized as her dad moved protectively closer to her and grabbed the colt's reins. Even more upset, Champion reared, towering over Ian.

As Champion reached higher and higher with his front hooves Cindy felt a strange sensation of floating into the sky, as if she had been released from gravity. Then she realized she was slipping. If Champion didn't go down, she was going to fall on her back.

142

And so might he, she realized in terror. *He could fall on me and we could both break our backs!*

Ian pulled sharply on the reins. Caught off balance, Champion toppled and struck him on the head.

"Dad!" Cindy screamed. She pulled hard on Champion's left rein, trying to make the colt fall away from her father. Even if she lost her balance and fell with Champion, she couldn't let his full weight come down on her dad.

"I'm all right!" Ian quickly rolled away from Champion's hooves. He got up, rubbing his head.

Champion came down to the ground with a thud. Cindy almost slid off to the side, but at the last second she grabbed his mane and stayed on. Despite her fright and the blur of events, she was determined not to fall. Falling would just tell Champion that anytime he didn't want to behave, all he had to do was rear and be rid of his rider.

In an instant Ashleigh was at Cindy's side, gripping her leg to support her in the saddle. Cindy quickly shifted her weight to a more balanced position and gathered the reins.

"Got him?" Ashleigh asked.

Cindy nodded. "I should have been ready for that," she said grimly. "Dad, are you really okay?"

"He just caught me a glancing blow." Ian winced. "I think I'm going to have a headache, though."

Champion was blowing hard and bowing his head

against the restraint of the reins. Cindy kept a close eye on him.

"I don't think he meant to do that," Ashleigh said. "He just got excited and struck out."

"I wasn't paying close enough attention to him," Ian said ruefully. "I was so worried about Cindy."

Cindy relaxed her grip on the reins just a little. She wondered if her dad was right to be worried. *What is Champion trying to do?* she thought. *There's only one way to find out.* "Let's take him in the gate again," she said.

"Absolutely not." Ian shook his head. "Get off him right now. You'll break your neck."

"No, I won't." Cindy wasn't at all sure of that. But she knew she had to keep trying with the colt. If Champion couldn't pass the gate test, he wouldn't be able to race at all. "Just once more," she promised. "I'll get right off if he acts up."

Ashleigh looked up at Cindy, her hazel eyes full of concern. "Are you sure you want to do this?" she asked.

Cindy nodded. "I have to," she said. Cindy felt bad for her dad. He had stepped back to allow her to try Champion again in the gate, but Cindy knew it was hard for him to watch her be in so much danger.

She started to firmly press her heels into Champion's sides, but then she stopped. *Wait a minute—calm down and figure out what to do*, she ordered herself. *No one can force Champion to do anything.*

He's bigger than all of us, especially me, and he's going to win if I fight with him.

Champion had stopped looking at Glory and was gazing backward at her. "Let's do it together, boy," she said simply. *That's the only way*, she realized. Cindy lightly lifted the reins, and Champion walked into the gate. Cindy nodded, and Ashleigh and Ian closed the gates.

Champion trembled with tension. Slowly Cindy reached forward to stroke his neck. "Hey," she said softly. "It's just me up here. You're doing fine, boy."

Cindy tried to stay calm. The tight gate was cozy with just herself and Champion inside, walled off from the world. After a few moments she thought she could feel Champion relaxing, too.

"That's enough for today." Ian opened the gate, and Cindy backed Champion out.

"Nice work, Cindy," Ashleigh said, nodding. "That was just fine—for a minute. But consistency is definitely not his strong point."

"I know." Cindy frowned. She knew it was probably a miracle or a fluke that Champion had behaved so well just now.

"Let's keep after him." Ashleigh studied the colt, frowning. "Maybe by the Breeders' Futurity we can get him straightened out."

Even Ashleigh doesn't sound sure, Cindy thought. *It's no wonder, after what Champion did to Dad.*

She looked at the colt. He was watching the track, where Vic and Philip were exercising a couple of the three-year-olds. "Those horses don't have nearly the talent you do, boy," Cindy said. "But they're doing better than you are. After today I'm definitely the only friend you've got left. And I'm not sure even I understand you sometimes."

That evening Cindy went down to the mares' paddock to help Len and Mark bring in the mares and foals. Cindy always loved dusk at the farm. This evening, the waning light had turned the fingers of clouds a soft violet. The air was filled with the warm smells of grain and hay, the whickers of horses eager for their dinner, and the sweet scent of mown grass.

Honor Bright and Princess were waiting with Wonder at the gate. Princess and Wonder were the dominant mares of the group, and so they were always the first to go up to the barn. "Hi, you guys." Cindy tickled Honor's nose. The beautiful little filly carefully sniffed her fingers, as if she were memorizing their scent. Or maybe, Cindy thought with a smile, Honor was hoping her fingers would turn into carrots!

Cindy clipped a lead rope to Princess's halter and slowly led the mare toward the barn, with Honor trotting at her heels. Cindy was pleased that she was the only person Ashleigh trusted to take Princess up to the barn. The mare's leg would always be fragile from the double break she had suffered a few years ago.

"Cindy!" Ashleigh hurried over to the paddock. "I wanted to tell you the news right away—we found out what's wrong with Mr. Wonderful."

"You did?" Cindy stopped dead, her heart filling with a mixture of happiness and fear.

"Mr. Wonderful has a viral infection." Ashleigh reached for a lead rope hanging from the gate and clipped it to Wonder's halter. "The infection was very low grade for a long time. But now it's flared up." Ashleigh shut the gate behind Wonder and fondly stroked the mare's shoulder.

"Is Mr. Wonderful going to be okay?" Cindy asked. Her heart was thumping. *Please don't let him die*, she prayed.

"He'll be fine," Ashleigh assured her. "Sometimes these infections can be tricky to detect. But now that we know what we're dealing with, we can treat it."

"That's so great!" Cindy let out a big sigh of relief. "Are you going to race him again?"

"We'll see," Ashleigh said. "A few of the owners and breeders I've talked to don't seem to feel that his value at stud is compromised by his recent losses at the track, now that we've discovered the cause. I don't know, Cindy." Ashleigh shook her head. "Mr. Wonderful is almost five, and it would take a while to bring him back. We'll keep evaluating his condition and make a final decision about racing him once we're sure he's healthy again."

"This is the best news ever," Cindy said. She turned to Honor. "Isn't it, girl?" Honor was standing at Princess's side, staring hard at Cindy as if she were trying to follow every word of the conversation.

Ashleigh grinned. "I couldn't feel better. Well, let's get these guys up to the barn."

So Ashleigh finally got to the bottom of the mystery of why Mr. Wonderful wasn't doing well at the track, Cindy thought happily as she put Princess and Honor in their roomy stall. *I bet I can find out why Champion acts the way he does, too.*

"Hurry," Cindy said, panting as she and Heather rushed down the hall at school the next afternoon. "We're going to be late for class."

"At least we know where we're going these days," Heather said with a giggle.

"That helps." Cindy didn't want to be late to science, one of her favorite classes. But she had been thinking nonstop about Champion all day, and she had dawdled at lunch, talking to Heather about the colt. Heather couldn't figure out why Champion was so on-again, off-again, either, but Cindy felt better just having someone to talk to about it.

"We can talk some more at my house when we work on our history project," Heather said. She and

Cindy were partners on a ten-page report about early American presidents. Cindy planned to go straight home with Heather after school.

"Sounds good," Cindy said. She parted from Heather at the gym and ran down the hall toward her science class.

Suddenly she slowed her steps. Max was walking ahead of her. "Uh-oh," she said under her breath.

Cindy stopped so that Max would go into his class before she reached him. That way they wouldn't have to talk. But Cindy felt a sharp pang of regret. Before they'd argued, she would have hurried to catch up with him.

I still can't believe we aren't talking anymore, she thought sadly. Cindy hadn't been able to share with Max any of her impressions of starting high school or tell him about her problems with Champion. She and Max had avoided each other for weeks. The dance was coming up that Friday.

I really can't blame Max for being mad, she realized. *I wasn't very nice about the dance. I was so sure things would go wrong before we even got there.*

"Wait a minute," Cindy said aloud, stopping in her tracks. She sank slowly to the floor with her back against a locker. Images of Champion flooded her mind. Champion twisting to see her one last time before he went out on the track for the Bashford. The colt's quick, positive response during workouts when she was happy. All the times Champion had been such good company at Storm's grave, but she had barely noticed him.

Cindy's mind was whirling. "I've been treating Champion just the way I've been treating Max," she murmured. "I don't expect Champion to behave well. I don't think he's as good as Storm. And Champion's so smart, he's figured it out. That's why he acts up."

The halls were nearly empty, but a couple of kids turned to stare at her. Cindy knew she must look crazy, sitting in the hall and talking to herself. Cindy almost laughed out loud. *Then they'd really stare!* she thought.

She couldn't care less. Her explanation for Champion's behavior was simple, but Cindy was sure she was right. It just felt right. Now all she needed to do was try it out.

13

Max was almost to his classroom. "I've got to apologize to him," Cindy murmured. "Or should I think some more about what to say? No, I'm sure I'm right about Champion *and* Max! Hey, Max!"

Max didn't turn, but Cindy was sure he'd heard her. He walked a little faster down the hall.

"Max, wait!" Cindy hurried after him and caught up to him just as he was about to go into the classroom.

Max turned slowly. "What do *you* want?" he asked.

Cindy hesitated. Max looked so mad, she was almost afraid to open her mouth. She hated the thought that they might have another fight.

Just tell him, she ordered herself. Even if Max was still angry after she apologized, she knew she would feel better for having tried. "I just wanted to tell you that I'm really sorry . . ."

"For what?" Max glanced into the classroom. He wasn't going to make this easy.

"For being a jerk," Cindy admitted. "I wasn't fair to you at all about the dance."

Max scrutinized her with his bright green eyes. "What do you mean?"

"Well, for some reason I assumed we wouldn't have a good time," Cindy said shyly. "But I shouldn't have thought that."

"Why?" Max was looking at her hard.

"I thought . . . it would be like I was going to the dance as your girlfriend," Cindy confessed. "And I'd feel—"

"What gave you that idea?" Max asked. He sounded surprised.

"The way you acted when you asked me to the dance. You seemed so embarrassed." Cindy scuffed the linoleum floor with her toe. "I really want to go. But it's different from going riding together."

"I know." Max nodded. "I thought about that, too. I mean, all the other kids in our class will be there. They'll see us, and they might talk about us. But I decided I don't care."

"Me either," Cindy said quickly. "As long as we feel okay about going with each other. As long as we're not . . . well . . ."

"I know what you mean," Max said. "I really like you a lot, Cindy. And I wanted someone to go to the dance with. But I'm not interested in you as a girl-friend. I still want to talk about horses, not about falling in love."

"That's good," Cindy said, laughing with relief.

Max put out his hand. "Friends?"

"Friends." Cindy shook his hand.

"Hey, Cindy," Max said. "Can I ask you just one more thing?"

"Sure." Cindy looked at him, puzzled.

Max grinned crookedly at her. "Do you want to go to the dance with me?"

Cindy smiled. "You bet," she said, and this time she meant it.

She glanced into the classroom. Mrs. Saunders, Max's photo-lab teacher, was still shuffling the papers on her desk around. "Can I tell you an idea I have for getting Champion to run better?" Cindy asked quickly.

"Sure," Max said, leaning against the wall. He seemed as glad as she was to have the misunder-standing cleared up.

"This sounds kind of nuts, but I don't think more practice or work is what Champion needs." Cindy bit her lip, thinking hard. "Champion's so smart, he knew exactly what Ashleigh, Dad, and I wanted him to do the first time in the gate and on the track. He just needs to know that it's wrong to act up—that I think it's wrong. But more than that, he needs to know I love him and trust him."

"Why not try to show him that?" Max suggested. "It can't hurt."

"I will." Cindy nodded decisively. "First thing tomorrow morning."

Before sunrise the next day Cindy walked down the training barn aisle to collect Champion. If Ashleigh approved, Cindy intended to take him to the track. Ashleigh had been out of town yesterday evening, and so Cindy planned to tell Ashleigh her new thoughts about Champion's training now.

Champion stood crosstied in the aisle, waiting for her. Cindy had told Len of her plan the night before, and he had fed Champion early and groomed the colt for her. The colt's almost black eyes were alert in his dark face as he watched her walk toward him. He was already quivering with eagerness to get going.

"You're definitely a morning horse, the way some people are morning people," Cindy said, running a hand down Champion's chocolate neck. "You couldn't look more gorgeous, boy. Let's show everybody today how well you can work."

"Ready?" Len asked, rolling a wheelbarrow down the aisle. He winked. "Good luck out there."

"Thanks—but I'm not sure yet if Ashleigh will let

us do this." Cindy glanced down the barn aisle to the office, where a light shone out the open doorway. Ashleigh was already at work, as she was every morning before sunup.

"She will." Len nodded reassuringly. "She wants Champion to run just as much as you do."

"I know. I'll go talk to her right now." Cindy unclipped Champion from the crossties and led him down the barn aisle. The colt followed quickly, his shod hooves ringing on the concrete.

Cindy looked into the stable office. Ashleigh sat at her computer, frowning at a list of feed expenses. "Morning," Cindy said. Champion looked in the doorway, too, propping his head on Cindy's shoulder as if he were prepared for a long conversation.

"What's up, Cindy?" Ashleigh took a sip of coffee from her mug. "Do you want to try Champion in the gate again? I can help you in a few minutes as soon as I finish going over these invoices."

"No, I didn't want to try the gate today. I was thinking . . ." Cindy hesitated. "If it's okay with you, I'd like to work Champion."

Ashleigh looked at her in surprise. "Are you sure?" she asked. "He really gave you a wild ride in the gate the last time you were on him."

Suddenly Cindy wasn't sure at all. If her theory about Champion—that he needed less discipline and more love and confidence from her—was wrong, the colt would act even worse under less restraint. She could be in for a dangerous ride.

Positive thinking, she reminded herself. "I wanted to try a new way of riding him," she said. "I've expected trouble with him so much, I wondered if I helped *make* the trouble. So today I'll keep him on a looser rein and try to believe in him."

Cindy could feel her face reddening. She knew she didn't have much experience as a trainer. *Ashleigh's trained Thoroughbreds for years*, Cindy thought. *My idea sounds so far-fetched!*

But Ashleigh nodded. "It's worth a shot," she said. "I'm not sure I trusted myself to have confidence in Champion, either. I was so disappointed when Mr. Wonderful's career came to an end, just when he had really moved into the big leagues. I guess I didn't want to get hurt again if things didn't work out with Champion, too. I always love Wonder's offspring so much." Ashleigh gave a little smile. "Maybe neither of us has been giving Champion the treatment he needs. So let's try him again today."

"Did you hear that, Champion?" Cindy said happily. Startled, the colt yanked his head from her shoulder and stared at her. Impulsively Cindy hugged him. "I can't wait to ride!" She had never meant anything more.

I really haven't been fair to him, she thought as she led the eager colt to the track. *Champion is inexperi-*

enced, and he's made some mistakes during his works and races. But I have to remember that he's not Storm, or Wonder, or any of the other horses. He's just himself, and that's one incredible colt.

At the gap Cindy stopped Champion to wait for Ashleigh. The black of night had barely given way to the deep, dim gray of dawn. The far side of the track, where Champion would run, was shrouded in mist. Cindy stood quietly, clearing her mind of all the past track disasters with the colt. Today they would make a new beginning.

The colt cautiously put his nose to her hair and took a deep sniff, then bobbed his nose at the track. He seemed to be saying that he was willing to try again if she was.

"Don't worry, boy," Cindy said confidently. "I'll prove to you that I mean what I say."

In a few minutes Ashleigh joined them and gave Cindy a leg into the saddle. "Put him through the usual warm-up paces and see what happens," she said. "We'll go on from there. I know that's what I almost always say with him, but you're going to make the difference today."

Cindy nodded, her eyes already turned to the track. "I'll try."

Champion set off at a brisk walk, his long, slender legs swiftly covering ground. Cindy started to take up on the reins to slow the colt, then stopped herself.

I bet I usually take up on him too soon, she thought. *I should try to control him more with my seat and voice.*

Cindy leaned back in the saddle. "Slower, Champion," she said quietly.

The colt flicked back an ear but continued to walk at the same quick pace. *Don't pull on him yet—give him time to respond*, Cindy reminded herself. *Trust him.*

After a moment Champion dropped his pace. "Wow! That's it!" Cindy patted his neck triumphantly.

Champion flicked back both ears, arching his neck and rolling his prominent eyes to look first at Cindy, then back at the track. His muscles bunched as Cindy moved him into a trot. "I'm controlling a lot of power," she murmured. "But I *am* keeping you under control, Champion. That's the point."

"You look good!" Ashleigh said as Cindy and Champion passed the gap for the first time. "Gallop him a lap slowly, then we'll see about increasing the pace."

"I think this is working!" Cindy smiled broadly. But she knew the real test would be when she asked Champion to run.

The sun's first rays were just shining over the hills, turning the mist yellow. At Cindy's voice signal the colt leaped into a gallop, his strides even and sure. In no time they had circled the track again.

"All right," Ashleigh called as Cindy approached

the gap again. "If you're okay with it, Cindy, gallop him to the three-eighths pole, then work him to the gap."

"I'm fine!" Cindy called. She decided not to stop and break the colt's rhythm. She could feel Champion's smooth, seemingly unlimited power at the quick pace of the gallop. His hooves dug evenly into the soft dirt, springing back up into long, airborne strides. *I won't have any problem today if I remember how to handle him,* she thought. *I could never control him by brute force anyway. And I can't trick him. With a horse as smart as Champion, he has to want to do what I say.*

Cindy fought off her last trace of misgivings. She tried to forget how badly Champion had gone for Ashleigh in his last race, only four days ago. *Champion's smart,* Cindy reminded herself. *He'll know what I'm trying to do.* But she knew that the big question was whether he would be willing to do it.

Cindy looked ahead to the three-eighths pole. The mist was lifting under the heat of the rising sun, and she could see clearly across the track. "Okay, Champion," Cindy said firmly. She took a deep breath, steadying herself over the colt's withers. "This is it!"

The three-eighths pole flashed by just as the sun exploded over the horizon, drenching the track in deep pink and yellow light. "Now, boy!" Cindy cried, moving her hands up on the colt's neck and burying them deep in his thick mane. "Run with all you've got!"

Champion changed leads and roared into a fast gallop, thundering down the track. The pace was so quick, the wind blew Cindy back in the saddle. Straightening, she gripped the colt's mane even tighter. Champion threw back his head and Cindy turned up her face, too, basking in the sharp wind tinged with the first coolness of fall. *This is absolute heaven!* she thought.

The sensitive colt veered slightly toward the rail, and Cindy felt a sharp flicker of fear. He was going out of control again! *I can't let him get away from me,* she cried silently.

"No!" Cindy called, sitting back a little. At the same moment she eased back on the reins, communicating through her hands, seat, and voice, with every ounce of will she had, that he couldn't act that way again. *I've got to let him know I've got confidence in him—and that I love him!*

The colt hesitated. Then Cindy could feel him responding. His entire body straightened again, and his strides evened out. Cindy leaned over his neck, pressing her cheek against his mane.

Suddenly Champion lunged ahead. He was moving so fast, Cindy could hardly separate the sound of his driving hoofbeats. But his gallop was still free flowing and effortless. "That's it, boy," Cindy cried. "You're doing your superdrive. Oh, wow! I can't believe this!"

The whipping wind and joy took Cindy's breath away as Champion hammered down the stretch. She had never felt such power and freedom as she rode a horse. Suddenly all Champion's strength and willfulness were channeled into the will to excel—the will to win!

At the gap Cindy stood in her stirrups, asking Champion to slow. "That's the way a racehorse acts," she praised, breathless with delight. The colt obeyed, but he was shaking his head with displeasure. He seemed to be saying, Why stop now, when things were going so well?

Cindy sat back in the saddle and posted to the trot. Her face was flushed from their effort and happy pride. *It's really possible he's some kind of miracle horse,* she thought.

"All right, Cindy!" Samantha called.

Cindy looked over at the gap and saw that she, Ashleigh, and Champion weren't alone anymore. Ian; Mike, holding baby Christina; Beth and Kevin; Len; and all the other stable hands stood at the rail. The onlookers erupted in cheers.

"They've got something to cheer about, don't they, boy?" Cindy was laughing with sheer delight as she dismounted. She rubbed Champion's nose, looking straight into the colt's intelligent eyes. "In two weeks you're going to take the field by storm in the Breeders' Futurity," she said. "What could stop us now?"

14

LATE FRIDAY AFTERNOON HEATHER CAME OVER TO CINDY'S house to get ready for the dance that night. "I'm so glad Doug asked you to the dance," Cindy said as she let her friend inside the front door. "Now we can go together."

"*I* asked *Doug*, remember?" Heather giggled. "Boy, that was the hardest thing I ever did in my life. I can really sympathize with Max for getting nervous when he asked you. I mean, what if Doug had said no? I would have really been crushed," she said more seriously.

"No one could say no to you two tonight," Samantha joked, coming in from the kitchen.

Beth was right behind her. "It's five-thirty, girls," she said. "Shall we head up to the bathroom and start on your hair and makeup?"

"I guess so. Are you coming?" Cindy asked Samantha. Cindy could feel butterflies starting in her stomach. Getting herself ready for a dance didn't seem nearly as easy or natural as tacking up a horse. "You have to come up to the bathroom and tell me if Beth goes overboard with the hairdo and makeup."

"I wouldn't miss it," Samantha said with a smile. "But I'll just be there for moral support—I'm not too handy with a curling iron."

In the bathroom Beth sat Cindy and Heather on stools and plugged in the curling iron.

"Don't make me look different," Cindy fretted. "I'll be embarrassed if everyone stares at me."

"Cindy, no one is going to be staring at you," Beth said as she expertly caught a lock of Cindy's hair with the curling iron. "Or if they do, they'll think you look lovely. The point is to make you look special for tonight."

Cindy was unconvinced. "I just want to blend in with the crowd," she said.

Ashleigh looked in the doorway. "This bathroom is crowded, but I couldn't resist stopping by. Wow, your first high school dance! I just had to see how you guys looked."

"Better than usual, I guess. But I wish I looked like you." Cindy glanced enviously in the mirror. Ashleigh had always been Cindy's ideal of perfection.

"Don't be silly, Cindy," Ashleigh said quickly. "You're a pretty girl. Don't sell yourself short."

Cindy stared at herself in the mirror. Her light brown eyes, flecked with darker brown, stared back. She had to admit that the curl Beth was adding to her hair made it frame her face, accentuating its oval shape and her cheekbones.

"Max will think you look just beautiful," Beth said firmly. "The same goes for Doug, Heather."

Cindy caught Heather's eye and winced. That kind of comment made Cindy think she wouldn't even have the courage to leave the cottage, never mind go to the dance. What would happen when all the kids at school saw her? Heather looked nervous, too, as if she were thinking the same thing.

An hour later they were carefully climbing into Ashleigh's car, trying not to step on their dresses. Ashleigh had volunteered to drive them to the dance. "I promise to be a good chauffeur and not say anything embarrassing," she said with a laugh.

"That's okay. I really appreciate your driving us," Cindy said. They had arranged with Max and Doug to meet them at the Smiths'.

"I feel weird," Heather whispered as she tucked her dress underneath her.

"So do I—but I think it's a good kind of weird," Cindy whispered back. "At least so far."

Cindy touched the soft cotton of her sky blue

dress, the color of Whitebrook's racing silks. She had bought it with Samantha last weekend. The style of the dress was simple, but the long, clean lines made her look taller and, according to Samantha, elegant. Cindy hoped the dress was right for a special night and that Max would think so, too.

The boys were waiting in front of the Smiths' house. Cindy swallowed hard, praying she wouldn't feel too awkward. Max and Doug hurried to the car and climbed in the backseat with Cindy and Heather.

"Hey, you look great." Max smiled.

"Thanks—so do you," Cindy said shyly. The dance was semiformal, and so Max wore a dark suit that went well with his dark hair, and a pressed white shirt. Cindy realized she had never seen him before in anything but jeans and casual shirts. *He looks different, but I think I like it*, she decided.

"Cindy rides Wonder's Champion," Heather told Doug.

"That's pretty incredible," Doug said to Cindy

"Thanks," Cindy said. She knew Doug slightly from her history class, but she had never really spoken with him. Doug had thick blond hair and bright blue eyes, like Heather. They looked almost like brother and sister.

"My dad told me about Champion. My dad's an assistant trainer at Clearview Acres," Doug said, naming a well-known Thoroughbred breeding and training farm. For the next ten minutes Cindy, Heather, Max, and Doug talked about horses. She almost forgot they were going to a dance.

"I'll pick you up at ten-thirty," Ashleigh said as she stopped the car in front of the school. "Have fun!"

"We will." Cindy quickly got out of the car with her friends.

"The gym's all lit up!" Heather pointed. Bright light streamed out the doors, and floodlights illuminated the exterior of the gym.

"Yeah, it's funny to be at school at night." Cindy strode toward the gym, trying to tame her nervousness.

"Hey, wait up!" Max called.

Cindy stopped to let Max, Heather, and Doug catch up. She remembered what Ashleigh had told her about the time when she was at a dance and her shyness had been mistaken for unfriendliness. Cindy didn't want her friends to think that about her.

"This place doesn't look bad," Max commented as the four of them walked into the gym.

"Thanks," Cindy said with a grin. She and Heather had been on the decorating committee again, although Cindy had only been able to make time for a couple of meetings. The theme of the dance was an enchanted forest in the fall. Dozens of tinsel red, orange, and yellow leaves drifted across the floor and caught the light. Heather had painted a backdrop of trees loaded with apples and nuts.

For once I'm not just admiring my work while I stand behind the punch table, Cindy thought. *I really get to enjoy it!*

"Hi, you guys!" Melissa waved to them from the refreshment table.

"Let's get something to drink," Max suggested.

"Sounds good." Cindy threaded her way through the crowd to the refreshment table. The large room was filled with the sound of a popular tune played by a live band.

"This is a really nice dance," Melissa said. She was with her date, Steven Wagner, who was a sophomore.

"Isn't it?" Cindy agreed, glancing around. Students were gathered in small groups, talking and laughing. The biggest group was around the refreshment table, which was loaded with vegetables, chips, and dip. At the center a huge crystal bowl was filled with fruit punch.

Cindy sipped the cup of punch Max handed her. She saw a few people she knew from her classes, but most of the students were in the higher grades at the school. Cindy started to relax. *This is no big deal,* she told herself. *I'm handling things just fine!*

Suddenly the lights dimmed almost to darkness, and the band began to play a song with a lively beat.

"This is a great song," Max said. "Do you want to dance?"

Cindy gulped. All her newfound confidence evaporated. "Um, I guess . . ." Cindy stared at her shoes. Even in the dark she knew her face was turning red. *How can I tell Max I don't really know how to dance?* she thought. Last night Samantha had tried to show her a few steps in the living room, but that was Cindy's only dancing experience. *Max is going to be sorry he asked me here,* she said to herself. *He should have asked someone who isn't such a klutz.*

"I can't dance very well," Max said. He grinned. "But I'll try if you will."

Cindy smiled back, feeling better. "I can't really dance at *all*, but let's go."

Max took her hand and led her out onto the dance floor. Cindy stood opposite him and tried to remember what Samantha had showed her. To Cindy's surprise, staying with the beat of the music wasn't that hard. She felt self-conscious about dancing in front of everyone. But after a few minutes she realized that Beth was right—everyone else was busy concentrating on their own partners and dancing.

In the subdued light Heather's silvery trees seemed almost alive, and the tinsel leaves glittered as they softly rustled across the floor. The effect was magical, Cindy thought with a happy sigh.

She bumped into Max. "Sorry," Cindy said. She giggled when she remembered Samantha's advice about dancing with a partner. "Just pretend he's a horse you have to stay with," Samantha had told her.

"What's so funny?" Max asked. He laughed when Cindy retold Samantha's joke.

Cindy danced several dances. She knew she wasn't a great dancer yet, but she thought this was something she could do if she worked at it.

Heather danced by with Doug. From the sparkle in Heather's eyes Cindy could tell that her friend was having a great time, too.

The band began a slow song, and the couples drew closer. "I don't think I'm quite ready to slow dance," Cindy said.

"Me either," Max agreed. "Let's just watch."

But after the slow song was over, Cindy couldn't wait to get back on the dance floor. Soon she and Max were inventing their own steps and laughing. They danced almost every dance.

"It's time to go," Max said a few hours later. He pointed to the clock in the gym.

"Is it really?" Cindy glanced at the clock. She couldn't believe how fast the hours had flown by. "We'd better go outside and look for Ashleigh." Cindy waved across the gym floor to Heather and gestured at the clock. Heather nodded to show that she understood.

Ashleigh was waiting in her car in the parking lot. "How did it go?" she asked.

"Just fantastic," Cindy said simply as she got into the backseat with her friends. *It's hard to believe I didn't want to come to the dance,* she added silently. *Now I wish this evening didn't have to end!*

Max looked over at her and smiled, seeming to know what she was thinking. "Thanks for coming to the dance with me," he said softly. Heather and Doug were talking quietly.

"We should go to another one." Cindy smiled back. The magic of the dance wasn't ending after all, she realized.

Cindy settled back comfortably on the seat. She felt good about the evening and about the way things had worked out with Max. *I don't have to give up my friendship with him, but we can do new things together,* she thought. *We'll be better friends than ever.*

15

"SO YOU SEE, STORM, CHAMPION'S GOT A MAJOR RACE ahead of him." Cindy knelt by the gray colt's grave and leaned forward to breathe in the scent of one of Storm's sweet-smelling flowers. "I'm sorry I haven't been out here in a while. I guess it's been a couple of days, huh?"

Lately Cindy hadn't had time to visit Storm's meadow. She had been intensively training Champion for the past week, ever since she and Ashleigh had started him on his new regimen. Every morning Cindy walked, galloped, or worked the colt to prepare him for the Breeders' Futurity, in just over a week. Champion had been doing very well in training. Cindy smiled, remembering her ride that morning on the dark chestnut colt. Cindy had worked Champion with Sea Tide, an allowance horse. Coming into the stretch Champion had closed in on the other colt, but he had straightened out when Cindy asked him to. The next moment he had responded instantly when she called on him to go into his superdrive. Cindy had thrilled to the pace as Champion roared through a work of half a mile.

Lately I've been so busy at school, too, Cindy thought. Cindy's teachers were assigning more homework than they had at the beginning of the semester. She had also joined the ninth-grade social planning committee, which met once a week. They were already planning a Thanksgiving dance.

Every afternoon Cindy had been spending a couple of hours with Honor Bright and the other weanlings. Honor and the rest of this year's foals had been weaned a few days ago, and Cindy had wanted to be there for them. After the initial shock of separation from their mothers, the young horses had adapted to life on their own and were full of high spirits. Sometimes Cindy worked with Honor on the lead line, but often Cindy would just watch her graze or gallop around the paddock. Cindy loved the exquisite little filly more every day.

Cindy looked at Storm's flowers and felt a pang of sadness. *Am I starting to forget you?* she wondered. "I'd never do that," she whispered. "I came out here because I want you to know about Champion's next race. I think he's going to do so well in the Breeders' Futurity, Storm. We're going to be really proud of him."

A gust of wind blew a small cyclone of dead leaves across the meadow. They rattled across the grave and dropped around the flowers. Carefully Cindy removed the leaves until the grave was tidy again.

She sat back on her heels. "It's really fall, isn't it?" she asked. "Oh, boy, I wish you were here to see it!"

Cindy's heart wrenched with grief. *It's my first fall without Storm*, she realized. *Sometimes I wish time would just stand still—I don't want to go on without him*. "Soon your flowers will die in the frost," Cindy said sadly. "I wish they wouldn't, Storm. It'll look so bare out here." Cindy dropped her head into her hands.

The back of her neck tickled. Startled, Cindy jerked up her head and saw Ashleigh and Fleet Street. Ashleigh was holding the stocky black filly on a lead line. "Hi," Ashleigh said. "We thought we might find you here."

Fleet Street had backed off a step at Cindy's sudden motion and stood at a safe distance, her head cocked. "So that was *your* whiskers tickling me—I thought they were somebody's." Cindy stretched a reassuring hand out to the young horse. "You're such a pretty girl, aren't you?"

"She looks like her dam," Ashleigh said, patting the filly's smooth neck. "She's the same color as Fleet Goddess and even has the same small star. If Fleet Street has half of Fleet Goddess's spirit, I'll be more than happy."

174

"I think she will." Cindy knew that two of Fleet Goddess's foals were stakes winners.

"Champion wasn't pleased when I left him behind just now," Ashleigh said with a laugh. "He was running up and down the fence line. You might go see him."

"He's used to a lot of attention. I guess I should go walk him." Cindy frowned, gazing at Storm's grave. "I'll be there in just a second."

Ashleigh nodded understandingly. "See you in a bit."

Cindy watched as Ashleigh and Fleet Street walked back across the meadow toward Whitebrook. She turned back to the grave. "I've got to go," Cindy said matter-of-factly. "Champion needs me more than you do, Storm." Tears blurred Cindy's eyes. She remembered the days when Storm would have been waiting for her in the paddock, too.

But I've got Champion now, Cindy reminded herself. An image of the gorgeous colt, impatiently pacing the paddock, flashed into her mind. Just thinking about Wonder's spirited, rebellious son made her feel better. Champion, whether he behaved well or badly, was so alive.

"So are you, Storm," Cindy said softly. "It's just you're only alive in my memories now. But you're still part of everything I do."

Cindy chewed a piece of grass, thinking about how well things had gone with Champion that week. The colt still tested her from time to time on the track.

Sometimes he went too fast or bore in or out slightly. But she had always been able to get through to him since she had begun to trust him, and all his performances had been stunning.

I've been so happy this week with Champion, she thought. *I hadn't felt that good since Storm got sick. But I bet I know why. I feel about Champion the way I did about Storm. Champion knows now that I really love him.*

"That's what you're telling me, isn't it, Storm?" she asked. "I should have treated Champion that way all along."

A cool breeze rustled the long grass. Cindy leaned back on her hands, enjoying the perfect peace of the meadow. She felt that both horses were very much with her.

Cindy smiled and got up. Brushing off her jeans, she turned to go. "Thanks, Storm," she said. "You give good advice. Oh, boy, I still love you. You know that, don't you?"

In the evening Cindy walked down to the paddock to get Champion for his dinner. She had visited him in the afternoon, sitting on the thick grass in the paddock for over an hour while he grazed. Champion had come over to her often, taking time from his grazing to sniff her hands or jeans. Cindy had just enjoyed being with him on a beautiful autumn afternoon.

Now the setting sun had drenched the horizon in

the west a deep orange. Cindy peered into the growing darkness. "Champion!" she called.

The big colt was waiting for her. An almost black silhouette, he was standing perfectly still in the center of the paddock. In the next paddock the eleven weanlings were milling about at the top of a small hill. They were a dark pack against the deep blue of the sky.

Cindy smiled as Champion broke into a brisk trot and headed for the gate. Clearly he couldn't wait for her to bring him in. "I know, it's dinnertime," Cindy said, attaching a lead line to his halter. "But you ate grass all day, Champion. You can't be starving."

Stepping inside the paddock, Cindy ran both hands down Champion's sleek neck. For a moment she closed her eyes, enjoying the tangy coolness of the autumn breeze.

Cindy opened her eyes and looked at Champion. He was standing quietly with his nose lifted, as if he were enjoying the sunset, too.

"Let's try something," she said. "I can trust you completely now, can't I?"

Cindy unclipped the lead line and took a step away from the gate. "Come with me, boy," she urged.

Without a moment's hesitation the colt followed her. Cindy's heart lifted at Champion's lovely, graceful walk and his unquestioning affection for her.

"That's a good guy," she whispered. "I really think things will be okay now."

Cindy thought she felt eyes on her. Whirling, she saw that all the weanlings were lined up in a perfect row along the fence, as if they were being judged at a horse show. The young horses were too short to see over the fence, and so eleven pairs of bright eyes were gazing in between the boards. The weanlings seemed to be keenly interested in Champion's progress.

"Don't be jealous of Champion—pretty soon you'll be racehorses, too," Cindy said. She could hardly believe how quickly the time had passed since these weanlings were born. Some of the mares would have their next foals as soon as January, only a few months away.

Cindy sighed with happy anticipation. Ground Zero and Heavenly Choir, both stakes winners, had been bred back to Glory a month after their foals had been born this year. Their foals, Glory's first, would be born next January or February. *I was afraid I'd miss Storm too much this winter to enjoy it, but I guess I'm looking forward to winter after all*, she thought.

Champion whinnied softly, as if he were asking a question.

"Let's go up to the barn and get your dinner," Cindy said. She reattached the lead line to Champion's halter as she opened the gate. She trusted him, but if Len or her dad saw the colt without restraint, they would worry.

Cindy noted with amusement that the weanlings had moved along the fence with her to their gate. The gate rattled briskly as small noses eagerly pushed it. "Don't worry—Len and Vic will be out for you in a minute!" she called.

The barn, already glowing with lights, was warm and inviting. Cindy walked quickly toward it, keeping up with the hungry colt beside her. She loved to be in the stable at night. The stable would be bustling with the sounds of hungry horses devouring their hay, grain, vitamins, and minerals. Soon after dinner the sleepy weanlings would flop flat out in their stalls after a day spent playing. Even the stallions quieted down and rested.

"In you go," Cindy said, opening the stall door for Champion. Champion turned instantly, waiting for her to bring his dinner.

Cindy poured Champion's grain into his box and filled his hay net and water bucket. Then she stood next to him to watch as he dug in.

Len passed the stall with a bucket of feed. "Len, do you think Champion is calmer lately?" she asked.

"He does seem to be." Len poured the grain into Freedom's box and joined her at Champion's stall. "I think as he gets older, he's making more sense of things."

Cindy nodded. But she knew in her heart that age wasn't the only reason.

16

THE DEEP REDS AND GOLDEN YELLOWS OF FALL HAD touched the trees that surrounded the lovely old track at Keeneland, where the Breeders' Futurity, the last race in the Bonus Series, would take place. Cindy filled her lungs with the crisp fall air, smelling faintly of damp leaves. The seven horses in the field had just walked out onto the track for the post parade. Champion was last. Cindy leaned forward in her grandstand seat for a better look.

"I hope Champion's in a good mood," Samantha remarked.

"So far he's been almost an angel." Cindy tried to gauge Champion's mood. In the walking ring he had minded Len and Ian almost perfectly. That was lucky, Cindy knew. The track officials hadn't permitted Champion to be alone in the saddling paddock or walking ring for this race. At that point Ian and Mike had seriously discussed scratching him. Ashleigh had talked them out of it, but just barely. Ian and Mike had seen Champion's improved works recently, but they were still concerned about a paddock or track accident.

In the walking ring Champion had spooked from a photographer who had abruptly pushed forward to take a picture. But that hardly counted as acting up, Cindy decided. The colt had definitely been interested in the other horses around him in the saddling paddock and walking ring. But he had left them alone.

Cindy had been glad of the opportunity to look over the other horses. When Champion had always been the first horse out of the ring, she hadn't been able to size up the competition nearly as well. But as she had looked over the field today, she noticed an unsettling coincidence.

"Dad . . ." Cindy turned hesitantly toward Ian, who was sitting on the other side of Beth in the stands. "Did you notice that every single horse Champion had a problem with in the first three races of the Bonus Series is running in this race? Duke's Devil, Syncope, Cajun King, and Secret Sign are all out there."

"No, I hadn't made that connection." Ian frowned. "But it's not really that surprising Champion is

181

meeting up with those colts again. Several of them are prepping for the Triple Crown races in the spring."

"I didn't think you were still pointing Champion toward the Triple Crown. That would be so great if Champion could run in the Kentucky Derby!" Cindy smiled broadly.

"It would be wonderful, sweetheart," Beth said, leaning around Ian to pat Cindy's knee.

"I'm still considering it," Ian said. "We'll see how Champion does today, and we'll keep evaluating what we should do with him. He's definitely out of excuses."

"I know." Cindy glanced back out at the track. Champion was walking briskly clockwise, bowing his head as he asked for rein. Cindy knew that the other jockeys hadn't forgotten Champion's previous behavior any more than her dad had. When the other jockeys had mounted up in the walking ring, Shawn Biermont, Secret Sign's jockey, had glared at Champion. Cindy noticed that Shawn was keeping Secret Sign far from Champion.

What if Shawn tries to whip Champion again? Cindy thought fearfully. *Or what if Champion goes after those colts the way he did in the other races of the Bonus Series?* In Cindy's experience most horses had long memories, but Champion had the longest she had ever seen. She doubted if he had forgotten what had happened with those horses in the other races. Cindy felt butterflies begin to flutter fiercely in her stomach.

Today will be different, she told herself. *You have to have faith in Champion. He's been good so far.*

"I wish we'd been able to take Champion out alone in the walking ring one more time," Mike said. "He doesn't need any more reasons to be wound up."

"Well, the stewards' decision to allow the other horses out with him was fair, I suppose," Ian said with a sigh.

Cajun King, Syncope, and Duke's Devil were passing Champion on the track as the horses headed for the starting gate. For a moment Cindy couldn't see Champion. Because the track was a mile and a sixteenth around, the length of the race, the horses were starting at the finish line.

"Why are those colts so close to Champion?" Samantha asked.

Cindy had been wondering the same thing. At that moment Champion's ears went back a fraction. "Look out!" she cried, even though she knew no one on the track could hear her.

Duke's Devil stepped sideways, his ears pinned. "He's going after Champion!" Cindy gasped. "Just like Champion went after him in the Bashford." Champion definitely wasn't the only colt in the race with a good memory, she realized with dismay.

Ashleigh quickly urged Champion forward, but

the colt hesitated. Cindy could almost see him deciding what to do. "Go on, Champion!" Cindy said between clenched teeth. "Don't fight!"

To Cindy's utter relief, the colt responded to Ashleigh's commands. He walked on at a brisk pace. Duke's Devil's jockey pulled his colt firmly to the outside.

"That was close," Mike said. "Funny—so Champion wasn't the aggressor for once."

"That was still a near miss," Ian said, picking up his binoculars. "We may be in for trouble."

"Champion wasn't fighting; he was just warning Duke's Devil off because he got too close," Cindy said quickly. She didn't want her dad and Mike to give up on Champion so soon. "Champion didn't want to let Duke's Devil push him around," she added.

Samantha smiled. "He never does let anyone push him around."

"I know." Cindy tried to sound confident. She crossed her fingers for luck as she watched the one horse, a small bay named Forever Fine, load in the gate. She knew that even if Champion had a smooth trip in this race, he wasn't going to have an easy time of it. Forever Fine already had a good racing record, with wins in his maiden race and an allowance race at Turfway. Duke's Devil, who was loading in the two hole, had lost to Champion in the Bashford but had run away with a stakes race in his next start. Cajun King was the three horse. He had never finished worse than second in his two starts.

Cindy felt even more nervous. "Champion's not going to walk away with this race, is he?" she asked Samantha.

Samantha shook her head. "No, he certainly isn't. But don't look so worried, Cindy. Champion can hold his own—especially now that you and Ashleigh have changed his training regimen."

"I think so, too." Cindy noticed on the board that Champion was going in at odds of five to one, behind Cajun King. "Champion really should be the favorite today. He beat Cajun King by almost three lengths in the Juvenile Stakes."

"A lot of people think Cajun King is due for a victory after his second-place finishes," Ian said. "Also, Champion can't run the aggressive race he ran in the Juvenile Stakes. If he pushes other horses around today, he'll be disqualified."

Champion just has to run here the way he's been working at home, Cindy said to herself, fixing her attention on Ashleigh and Champion. *But first he has to load well in the gate.* Champion was about to go into the four slot. Holding her breath, Cindy tried to block out her bad memory of how Champion had almost thrown Ashleigh in the gate in both the Bashford and the Kentucky Cup Juvenile Stakes.

185

"The press are calling Champion a gate terror," Mike commented.

"That's not fair anymore—Champion passed his gate test last week with flying colors," Cindy argued.

"He sure did," Samantha smiled at Cindy reassuringly.

"There he goes, right in the gate without any problem," Ian said.

Now if he'll just stay on all four feet! Cindy half rose from her seat, trying to see the colt. *Hang on, Champion—it's only seconds until the bell rings.*

Cindy was thankful that the three remaining horses in the field quickly loaded. Then the stands were nearly silent as the crowd waited for the race to begin. Cindy could hardly bear the tension. She squeezed her hands tightly together, willing Champion not to lose his focus before the gate opened.

At last the bell shrilled into the quiet. Cindy jumped, even though she had been expecting the sound.

Champion broke cleanly from the gate, soaring onto the track. "Go, Champion!" Cindy cried. "That's the way!" But she saw that to Champion's outside, Syncope and Secret Sign had broken well, too.

"And they're off!" the announcer called. "It's Wonder's Champion by a nose over Syncope and Secret Sign. Antisan in fourth, followed by Duke's

Devil and Forever Fine. Back three to Cajun King as they head into the first turn."

Cindy half stood, straining to see. "Champion's falling back!" she cried. "But he's close to the rail."

"Ashleigh was going to try to rate him," Mike reminded her.

"So far, so good—I think," Ian agreed. "Champion's a closer, but I'm not sure I want him behind horses today. He might fight."

"Every race is so different," Beth said, sounding nervous.

"Jockeys have to wing it on the track," Mike agreed.

"And Ashleigh's the best," Cindy added. But she could hardly bear it when Champion was behind. Syncope was half a length ahead of Champion as the field pounded across the backstretch. The gray colt was still slowly increasing his lead over Champion.

The horses rushed into the far turn. Now the angle was better, and Cindy could see the positions of the horses clearly. "Syncope's bearing in and cutting Champion off!" Cindy cried.

"You're right." Ian quickly adjusted his binoculars. "Syncope is bearing in badly."

"Champion doesn't have anywhere to go. He's right up against the rail!" Cindy stared at the track. Even a glancing blow against the rail would put Champion out of the race or worse.

No, I was wrong—he does have somewhere to go! With a quick skip the dark chestnut colt changed leads and roared in front of Syncope.

"Yes!" Cindy shouted in triumph. Now Champion was on the lead, and Syncope was falling back. Probably the other colt had borne in like that because he was tiring, Cindy realized. Secret Sign was a length back and by no means out of contention. But the rest in the field were trailing. Cajun King, in third, was six lengths back.

"They're heading for home," the announcer called. "But here comes Cajun King! He's bearing down on the front runners like a rocket!"

Cindy could hardly believe her eyes. Cajun King was eating up ground faster than she had thought a horse could move. He ripped by Secret Sign and bore down on Champion. "Don't let him catch you, Champion!" Cindy cried. "Hurry!"

"I doubt if Cajun King can sustain that pace," Ian said.

Yes, he can! Cindy thought. Cajun King was almost at Champion's flank.

"Cajun King is slowing," Samantha said.

"No, I think Champion is going faster!" Cindy swallowed hard with excitement.

"Danny Rodriguez will have to take Cajun King around Champion—there isn't room on the rail for Cajun King to get through," Mike said.

"Look—Rodriguez is trying to go through on the inside after all," Samantha cried.

"Cajun King will never fit," Cindy said. Then she strained to see if she was wrong somehow. But as the two colts rounded the last bend of the far turn, Cindy could see just how close they were. *Champion squeezed through on the rail by Cajun King in the Juvenile Stakes*, Cindy remembered, her heart pounding. *Is Rodriguez doing this just to get even? It isn't going to work now!*

Champion wasn't giving up an inch of ground. Cindy could almost feel how hard the dark chestnut colt was battling to stay in front and on the rail. Slowly Champion began to draw off from Cajun King.

"Rodriguez thought he could intimidate our horse into giving up ground!" Mike shouted over the cheers of the crowd.

"Bad move—it didn't work," Samantha said.

"I don't think Danny Rodriguez had enough horse left to go around Champion any other way," Ian answered.

"Champion's going to win it!" Cindy exclaimed. She joyfully watched Champion gallop down the stretch, far ahead of the pack.

"We can't be sure of that yet," Ian said. "Secret Sign is closing!"

Cindy's heart sank as she saw Secret Sign power up to Champion. In barely seconds the other colt gained length after length, with no sign of tiring. *But Champion may be tired*, Cindy thought. *He's already had to run hard twice to stay ahead—when he pulled ahead of Syncope and to outrun Cajun King on the far turn.* One of those fast runs might have been Champion's highest gear. If so, Cindy knew he might not have anything left.

Secret Sign drew up on Champion's outside flank. For a moment Cindy thought Champion wouldn't be able to stop the other colt's surge to the lead. "Wait—there goes Champion!" she cried in delight. "Go, boy—you've got it!"

Champion reached for ground, but Secret Sign battled back, gaining on Champion until the two colts were almost neck and neck.

Champion suddenly staggered to the inside. "What happened?" Mike shouted. He sounded stunned. "Did Shawn whip Champion again?"

"I think Champion just jumped inside." Ian's voice was very worried.

"Champion thought Shawn would whip him again when Secret Sign got that close." Cindy's heart was pounding. "Champion's going to hit the rail!"

"Give him room to run, Shawn!" Mike said urgently.

Ashleigh was forced to check Champion hard. At the last fraction of a second Secret Sign's jockey moved his colt a bit to the outside. But Secret Sign was on the lead by half a length, and the wire was looming.

"I don't think Champion can win it now," Mike said.

"No, you're wrong!" Cindy could feel her heart soaring with Champion's strides. Ashleigh had quickly collected the colt, and he was flying in pursuit of Secret Sign.

"And it's Wonder's Champion, charging home!" the announcer said.

"He's caught Secret Sign," Cindy gasped. "Just run for it now, Champion!" *He's all by himself now,* she thought in wonder. *But he's still running faster with every stride!*

Alone on the lead, with his nearest rival four lengths back, Champion pounded to the finish. Moments later he flashed to victory under the wire.

"Wonder's Champion is the overpowering winner! And after a very troubled trip," called the announcer.

"Champion, you were so great!" Cindy was almost crying with happiness. She turned to her family. "Let's go tell him just how well he did!"

Mike grinned broadly. Cindy could tell from her dad's and Mike's expressions that they were just as proud of Champion as she was. *Finally everyone knows how talented he is,* she realized.

Ashleigh was riding up just behind Shawn Biermont on Secret Sign. Ashleigh was beaming, but the other jockey looked angry. *Tough luck,* Cindy thought. *Champion won, no matter what you tried to do to him!*

"Ashleigh, this is so fantastic!" Cindy ran to the colt's side. Champion was huffing out excited breaths and hopping lightly on his front feet. He dropped his head for a moment to affectionately nuzzle her hair.

"Isn't it?" Ashleigh jumped down out of the saddle, and she and Cindy hugged. "This is quite a victory!"

"Did Shawn hit Champion out there?" Mike asked. "If he did, I'm going to have another word with the stewards."

"No, Champion just jumped out of Secret Sign's way," Ashleigh said. She unfastened her helmet and took a deep breath. "Whew, I'm a little tired after that ride!"

"How did Champion win after so many things went wrong?" Cindy couldn't stop smiling. "He showed so much heart!"

"He did," Ashleigh agreed.

"He's my Champion," Cindy said, laughing with joy and relief. Every last bit of her doubt about the colt was gone. *I'm not sad anymore,* she realized. *Not even about Storm. He'd be happy for Champion, too.*

She hugged Champion tightly. The colt nudged her hard with his nose, then huffed out a contented sigh.

"I think he's shown everybody he's your Champion," Samantha said with a smile.

"He sure has!" Ashleigh agreed.

In the winner's circle Cindy held Champion's bridle with Ashleigh and faced the reporters and photographers. Samantha, Ian, Mike, and Beth gathered around them.

"Smile, everybody!" Cindy pressed her cheek against Champion's dark, silken mane. The colt's ears shot up, and he turned his head toward Cindy. "Thanks for that wonderful race, boy," she whispered. "I love you so much."

The beautiful colt tossed his head and leaned against her. He whickered softly, as if to say that he loved her very much, too.

JOANNA CAMPBELL was born and raised in Norwalk, Connecticut, and grew up loving horses. She eventually owned a horse of her own and took riding lessons for a number of years, specializing in jumping. She still rides when possible and has started her three-year-old granddaughter on lessons. In addition to publishing over twenty-five novels for young adults, she is the author of four adult novels. She has also sung and played piano professionally and owned an antique business. She now lives on the coast of Maine in Camden with her husband, Ian Bruce. She has two childern, Kimberly and Kenneth, and three grandchildren.

KAREN BENTLEY rode in English equitation and jumping classes as a child and in Western equitation and barrel-racing classes as a teenager. She has bred and raised Quarter Horses and, during a sojourn on the East Coast, owned a half-Thoroughbred jumper. She now owns a red roan registered Quarter Horse with some reining moves and lives in New Mexico. She has published eight novels for young adults.